CARRIE ▾ MERRILL

YOU
SHOULD
FEAR THIS
EVIL

S.P.E.C.T.E.R.

THE DEVIL'S PLAYGROUND

The Devil's Playground ~ *You Should Fear This Evil*
A Paranormal Suspense Thriller
S.P.E.C.T.E.R series, Book 2
by Carrie Merrill

Published by
    Christopher Matthews Publishing
    an imprint of First Steps Publishing (Oregon)
    FirstStepsPublishing.com

ISBN-13:
    978-1-945146-68-8 (hbk)
    978-1-945146-69-5 (pbk)
    978-1-945146-65-7 (epub)

The events, peoples and incidents in this story are the sole product of the author's imagination. The story is fictitious, and any resemblance to individuals, living or dead, is purely coincidental. Historical, geographic, and political issues are based on fact; the stories of the children of Central America are based on truth, however, the names have been changed to protect the innocent.

Every effort has been made to be accurate. The author assumes no responsibility or liability for errors made in this book.

Book & Cover layout & design by Suzanne Parrott
Purgatory Man (cover) ©Carrie Merrill / used with permission
Antigonish, William Hughes Mearns, 1899, (poem, p.117, Creative Commons)

Library of Congress Control Number: 2025920951
paranormal suspense thriller | ghost / horror | FBI | murder |
possession | supernatural | cult practices paganism

Printed and bound
in the United States of America.

To my siblings,
without whom
I wouldn't be this evil.

BOOKS BY CARRIE MERRILL

— S.P.E.C.T.E.R. Series —

The Lazarus Project
The Devil's Playground

— Angel Blade Series —

Angel Blade
Daemon
Archangel
Harbingers

*

The Key, the Outlaw and the Treasure
Time of Death

* * *

Follow Carrie Merrill at
CarrieMerrill.com

"The fury of a demon instantly possessed me.
I knew myself no longer. My original soul
seemed, at once, to take its
flight from my body..."

Edgar Allan Poe - *The Black Cat*

CHAPTER 1

Special Agent Ryan Mills watched the murder unfold like a ghostly replay, revealing every brutal detail. She knew that the killers may never be identified. Yet, there was satisfaction knowing that the victim would no longer remain buried in this desolate place.

"Special Agent Mills," a man called out from the small patch of green weeds and grass shaded by the surrounding birch trees.

Mid-morning sunlight burned around the edge of Ryan's sunglasses. She glanced up, the cell phone still to her ear, barely hearing Dr. Matt Holbrook's voice murmuring on the other end. Instead, her attention was fixed on a small plot of churned earth.

"I think we've got something." The crime scene investigator waved at her. Dark earth lay in piles around his feet, scattered across a bright blue tarp, ready for analysts to sift through for evidence.

"Hey, Doc," she said, "I gotta go, but I'll call you back."

Although she couldn't see it, she could sense a satisfied smile spreading over his lips. "I knew it. I knew you were right," he said, the English accent thick in his voice.

The phone slipped away from her ear, and she absentmindedly pocketed it in one fluid motion. This is what she'd been waiting for.

She'd known the body was here for months, long before the cadaver dogs caught the scent in this empty grove at the edge of the woods. She'd always known. But none of these people would believe her unless she revealed the truth of her own thoughts. And she didn't need to because she was the lead agent of SPECTER—*Society of Paranormal Evaluation, Characterization, Testing, Experimentation and Research*—a classified division of the FBI.

She'd once aspired to be nothing more than a homicide detective. That was ambitious enough after growing up in small-town Montana. Then Holbrook entered her life and introduced her to SPECTER. Everything changed after that.

The first time she'd walked into that place, she knew her world would never be the same. The Lazarus machine could literally raise the echoes of the dead from the smallest trace evidence of a cold case. This was why SPECTER was created. But Holbrook noticed something more in Ryan—how she could *interact* with the device in ways no one else could.

Hunches, images that flashed in her mind, the way a crime scene whispered its secrets to her. It wasn't intuition, but something far more. Something she'd had since childhood.

Lazarus didn't merely support her instincts—it amplified them. Now, she could see what others couldn't. And sometimes, the dead spoke back.

Only Holbrook knew the full extent of her ability. He called her special, but she wasn't so sure. However, whatever this *gift* was, it had helped them find her sister's killer—and dozens more since.

She used to think her visions were hallucinations. Now she knew better. The dead didn't always rest quietly.

Hours earlier, the site had been cordoned off, and stakes

were used to anchor a white cord around the excavation site. Now, the crime scene investigator crouched within the plot, holding a small trowel and brush.

Here I am.

As Stephen Jeffries' voice whispered in Ryan's mind, the breath of his words blended with the tide of sounds churning within her, and a shiver prickled down her spine.

He'd waited fifteen years for this day—the day he could finally tell his story to everyone, not just to Ryan. He stood behind her, nothing more than a hidden mirage in the sunlight, and looked over her shoulder at the overturned earth.

Ryan's boot bent the weeds at the edge of the plot. She gazed down into the rectangular grave dug three and a half feet into the ground. Damp earth rose in the humid mid-west air, mixed with summer pollen and the electric buzz of cicadas.

In all the sounds and smells of the woods, a dirt-stained plate of bone peeked through the dark brown clumps of sandy clay. The analyst crouched and applied the brush in gentle strokes until the familiar curves and crevices of bone were revealed. As he cleared away more debris, a frontal bone, with the right orbital arch margin barely visible above the surface, caught the dappled sunlight that filtered through the leaves above the glen.

More than twenty-five years after his murder, Stephen Jeffries had been found.

Only a few feet of ground within the cordoned-off plot had been excavated, but Ryan knew the rest of the body was buried beneath the weeds. The same flickering images that had brought her here continued to replay in her mind like an old reel-to-reel movie. The victim's throat was cut nearly to the bone, his body hauled two miles by truck, and then dumped down a lonely, wooded side road. Thick weeds and a dead-end dirt road that stopped at the foothills made this the perfect place to hide a body.

The killers pulled two shovels from the back of the truck and dug the grave deep enough to hide the body and keep away anything natural that might reveal it. But they hadn't counted on the supernatural. The messages that had come to Ryan with the help of Lazarus, which hadn't existed when Stephen was murdered. Who could have guessed back then that Doc would invent something capable of recreating images of a cold-case crime scene from the slightest traces of evidence? And even Ryan never imagined it would awaken her abilities, driving her to this desolate place where she could actually see and hear Stephen. And to witness his bones in the ground now.

Ryan crouched at the edge of the border and followed the path of uneven ground behind the analyst. The images pulsed within her mind at a rapid pace, like a playback of a degraded film of Stephen's memories forcibly mingling with her own thoughts. It was his only way to communicate with her.

Acid burned at the back of her throat, and she swallowed hard when she witnessed the two killers pull Stephen's body out of the truck, his head slamming against the tailgate with a sickening thud. When they let the body fall unceremoniously to the ground in a heavy clump, her eyes stung with rage. They didn't care that Stephen had been alive ten minutes earlier. They didn't care that he was a human being.

The two men carried the body, one at his ankles and the other at his wrists, until they had reached the grave. The greasy man at his wrists winced when he dropped Stephen onto the ground, shaking and grabbing at his hand in pain. Then he angrily spat on the body.

Ryan glanced at the man's hand and then at the body. *He*

They rolled the body into the hole, and as his body lay there, staring blankly up to the moonless sky, one of them stood at the foot of the grave. He inhaled deeply on his cigarette. The smoke that billowed with his exhale made Ryan cough. The man smirked, pulling the cigarette from his lips as the smoke continued to trickle out of the corners of his mouth.

"Faggot," he mumbled and flicked the cigarette into the grave. It fell against Stephen's hip and rolled down until it settled against his still hand.

Before they had even begun to cover the body, Ryan blinked her eyes clear of the ghostly images, returning to the bright afternoon sunlight and familiar cries of cicadas. *Yes*, she thought. She now had everything that could bring justice to Stephen after all these years.

"Here." The analyst glanced back at her. Ryan's open hand hovered over the undisturbed ground at the edge of the border. "Dig here."

"But . . ." he said.

"Just do it." She didn't say it with anger, but everything in her stare meant that he needed to do it now.

The analyst didn't argue. The trowel plunged into the ground with careful scoops until the surface vegetation was broken enough to remove the top layer. Each scoop of dirt was placed into a bucket, where the other technicians sifted through it for trace evidence. Every minute that ticked by made Ryan's fist clench tighter.

"Okay," the analyst finally said, and he traded the trowel for his brush and a thin metal pick. "We've got more bone."

Whenever the brush came out, the dig slowed down. But it

also meant that something important lay under the surface. The brush removed debris in gentle sweeps, revealing small pieces of white bone.

"Phalanges," he called out to her. "And metacarpals."

"Anything else?" she whispered.

The analyst said nothing, his face only a few inches from the ground as he continued to sweep away thin layers of dirt.

"Wait a sec," he said, almost to himself. As he picked away layers around the hand bones, Ryan leaned in closer. "I see a ring." The soft edges of the brush smoothed around the curve of the ring. "It looks like a skull. And what appears to be degraded pieces of paper in the soil around the hands."

Adrenaline surged into her veins, causing her hands to tremble.

The analyst sat upright, glancing at her, his eyes wide. "It may be the remains of a cigarette."

She smiled and withdrew a clear evidence bag from her pocket. "I know. Swab carefully around the ring. You may find traces of someone else's DNA."

"Yeah," he said, and then his brow furrowed. "But how did you know these would be here?"

The bag crinkled in her hand as she held it open for him. "I'm that good."

He scooped out the paper remains and placed them into the evidence bag. Ryan sealed it and held it to the light. The butt of it was still there, dirty but complete. This could be the evidence she needed. DNA clung to that paper, and possibly a fingerprint.

Ryan stood. "Bag *everything* you find, including that ring. The FBI medical examiner will accept the remains at the forensics lab when you're done here." She turned away and headed toward her car.

"And what about you?" he called out.

"And then the remains get sent to my lab," she said. "That's where we catch these guys."

She climbed into the car and closed the door, shutting out the incessant insect sounds that had begun to burrow into her brain. Everyone stood next to Stephen's final resting place, including Stephen. Unseen and quiet. None of them would even know he looked down at his bones. But Ryan knew. She knew it in the same way she could still smell the killer's cigarette smoke as it clung to her hair and clothes.

As she sat behind the wheel of her car, Stephen looked up from the edge of his grave and met her eyes. The faintest hint of a smile played at the edge of his lips before he turned. As he slipped into the shade of the forest canopy, he disappeared.

The weight of Stephen's thoughts lifted from her mind, and she leaned back against the seat, waiting for one more. They had raced through her mind for months, but now, they were gone. Stephen was at peace, and she could finally let him go.

There were countless more back at the Lazarus lab, where Doc and the others waited. Cold cases filled a locked room where Director Price had made it very clear Ryan was in charge of solving as many as possible. Stephen Jeffries was only one of thousands, and new cases arrived every day.

She had no time to rest.

CHAPTER 2

"Honey, I'm home!" Ryan called, her voice echoing off the walls of the Lazarus lab. With a backpack slung over one shoulder, she entered the brightly lit entryway where rows of metal tables gleamed, each cluttered with Dr. Holbrook's technical equipment. Today, the sharp smell of solder and ozone filled the air.

Each step she took held deep satisfaction. Stephen would always hold a special place in her heart as the first ghost she encountered since joining SPECTER. A quarter-century old cold case shrouded in mystery that had almost reached a gratifying conclusion.

At the far end of the lab, Holbrook looked up from his workspace. Thick-lensed goggles magnified his eyes into two huge cartoonish orbs. A broad smile spread across his face.

"Special Agent Mills," he said, lifting the goggles up to his forehead, causing his hair to stand up even higher—the perfect picture of a mad scientist, complete with an English accent. Whatever he'd been working on lay abandoned when he stood, shoving his hands into the pockets of the slacks under the long white lab coat he wore. "Bravo, Agent. Congratulations on finding Mr. Jeffries' remains."

"Thanks, but we still haven't solved his case. We still need to find the murderers." She placed her backpack onto the table.

"But you found the body," he said with a slight bow. "That's something no one has managed to do in twenty-five years."

She slid her hand into the back pocket of her jeans and fished out her phone. "That's not the only thing." The screen lit up with the photo app, and she angled the screen toward him. "Found this next to him."

Holbrook scrunched his nose. "What is that?"

Ryan nodded. "Partial remains of a cigarette. I saw one of the killers drop it in the grave before they covered him. And Jeffries wore a ring. Forensics is running tests for DNA and prints. Even more evidence to corroborate with Lazarus once they send the body."

"Even better news." His smile widened.

She glanced down at the jumble of wires and electronics spread across the table surface. "What's going on here?"

"Oh, right," Holbrook said as his hands emerged from his pockets again. "A project I've been mulling over for a long time." Fingers toyed with the device at the center of the clutter. It resembled a gutted smartwatch with its face removed and inner wires exposed. "I've been experimenting with the technology I used in Lazarus. The idea is based on changing the polarity . . ."

After that, Ryan had no idea what he was talking about. Before long, he stopped and turned toward her.

"I've lost you, again, haven't I?" he said.

Her eyebrows rose. "Are you surprised?"

"I'll never underestimate you." A wink and a grin flashed across her face as Holbrook's fingers moved deftly over the watch until the black glass face clicked into place. "This is only a demo piece, but let me show you."

He pressed a small button on the side, and a circle of small LED lights appeared on the watch face, flashed a couple of times, and then disappeared. "You'd wear this on your wrist. It's designed to detect aberrational electromagnetic pulse waves."

Her brow furrowed. "Aberrational waves—random waves *not* generated by electronics. Waves that should otherwise not be there." Ryan nodded.

"Correct, Agent," he said with a hint of surprise. His fingers brushed the side of the watch again, and the lights started to cycle in a slow, clockwise direction—like a computer screen's spinning wheel when it was 'thinking.' "If you're within a few feet of an aberrant pulse, it will alert you and provide the proper orientation." The lights continued their steady rotation until three dots in a row flared a bright green.

"So, I just follow the green lights," Ryan said.

He nodded. "And when you're in the right spot," he paused when the circle of green lights stopped cycling and flashed in unison, "it helps us locate where mini-Lazarus is most likely to detect an embedded energy memory."

"Mini-Lazarus," Ryan said, her finger touching the face of the watch. "It's brilliant."

"Thank you." He leaned over the table until next to her shoulder and whispered, "I should have one for you by tomorrow."

Ryan nodded. Then exhaustion settled in her bones, and she took a step back from the table. It had been a long day. She hadn't even stopped at home after landing—came straight from the airport to the lab. Any more talk of complex electronics threatened to give her a headache.

"Is anyone else here today?" she said, glancing beyond Holbrook toward the main door to the Lazarus room.

His smile wavered, but it was too subtle for Ryan to notice. "Um, yes. I believe Dave and Coti are still working."

"Excellent. I want to share the good news about Stephen."

She clapped Holbrook firmly on the shoulder, then pushed through the doors into the dimly lit Lazarus room.

The faint amber glow emanating from the corners of the room did little to help her eyes adjust to the darkness. Bright computer monitors at the edge of the Lazarus machine illuminated the space, reflecting off Dave's glasses as he glanced up.

"Hey, Mills," Dave called from behind the monitor bank of the Lazarus mainframe. He spun his wheelchair around to face her. "You're back already." The latest program code he had been creating left his eyes bloodshot behind the glasses perched atop the bridge of his nose.

Coti's slender frame and short black hair emerged from behind the machine, wrench in hand and a smudge of grease on her chin. "Hey!"

Ryan nodded once to her. "What's going on with Lazarus today?"

Coti glanced down at the wrench and the dark smudges of carbon dust staining her knuckles. "Oh, nothing really. The usual blown fuses and replacing another fried circuit. Got it running like new again."

The door closed behind Ryan, blocking out the light from the entry lab and plunging the room into deeper darkness.

"So, how'd it go?" Coti asked as she walked across the machine platform.

Ryan grinned. "We found him! We found the body."

"I knew it," Dave said, his voice echoing throughout the room. "You did it."

"No," Ryan said as she stepped up beside him, nudging his shoulder with her hip. "*We* did it."

"I can't believe it," Coti muttered. "He's been in the Missing Persons vault for so long. Did you get to see his body?"

"Well," Ryan shrugged, her gaze falling to the dark floor. "His skull. And the left hand—at least, the bones of it."

Coti fell silent, and it was too dark to see her eyes. "He was all alone there for such a long time. And nobody knew."

"They will now," Ryan said. "And his killers won't be anonymous for much longer, not after we're done processing him."

"Well," Dave said, clearing his throat loudly. "This calls for a celebration."

Coti's voice brightened. "I agree."

"It's decided then," Holbrook's voice boomed from behind Ryan, and she turned to face him. "We'll meet at Gregario's in an hour. Drinks are on me."

"I still need to fix the cooling tower, genius," Coti interjected. "Lazarus overheats if we go over thirty minutes."

"Alright." Dave rolled his eyes and turned his chair to face the monitors. "Cooling tower first. Drinks afterward."

"It's a date," Holbrook said with a grin and a wink toward Ryan.

****

The music was so loud that Ryan couldn't hear most of what Coti said as she shared a story from across the table. Dave laughed, though, causing Coti to spill beer from her tall glass, making her laugh harder. A basket of buffalo wings had already vanished, and it would leave Ryan with heartburn by morning. But that didn't matter. Everyone smiled and sometimes sang along with the music. Even Holbrook joined in when a Spice Girls song filled the room. Coti said something to Dave, and they both headed to the dance floor, with him wheeling around her as they danced.

Ryan leaned across the table to Holbrook. "Won't his wife be jealous?" she shouted over the music.

He took a sip of beer, the foam clinging to his lips, which he wiped away with the napkin on the table. "Not at all. She's a lesbian; not his type at all."

Her eyes went wide. "Dave's wife?"

Holbrook laughed. "No. Coti. She loves to party, and his wife knows about her."

"I had no idea," she said, her fingers clutching a chilled bottle.

"And how about you?" he asked, taking another drink.

Those wide eyes shone again. "I'm not a lesbian."

Holbrook covered his mouth, nearly spraying his drink everywhere. After wiping his mouth again, he smiled. "I meant, do you want to dance?"

"I can't dance," she shouted above the fast beat.

"I can't either. Two left feet."

Ryan turned her gaze back to the dance floor and smiled as she watched Dave wheel around Coti.

"I have a proposition for you," Holbrook yelled above the music.

She turned to him. The music blared so loudly that her ears rang. "I can't hear you."

He ticked his head toward the side door. Everyone had been escaping that way when they wanted to smoke between songs before coming back inside. Holbrook didn't seem the type to take a drag, and Ryan had never smelled it on his clothes before, but she didn't mind stepping outside for some fresh air. She followed him out the door, and thankfully, nobody was out there puffing on cigarettes, so the air was clean.

Holbrook had left his long white coat in the lab and now

stood in the dark with the sleeves of his button-down shirt rolled up to the elbows. He brushed back the thick brown hair that sometimes flopped over his eyes.

"Ah, I can finally hear," she said, taking a deep breath.

"I wanted to ask you something," Holbrook said, leaning against the brick wall.

Her throat tightened as she gave him a sideways glance. "That sounds suspicious." Ryan hadn't spent enough time around Holbrook when he'd been drinking to know what to expect and wasn't about to risk saying something they'd both regret in the morning. He was a co-worker, perhaps even her best friend. After everything they'd been through over the past year, she'd do anything for him. But she wouldn't jeopardize their friendship over a drunken advance.

"Perhaps." He flashed her a grin. "There's a woman that I would like you to meet."

Her eyebrows rose. "Not what I was expecting to hear."

"After all the work we've accomplished with Lazarus, I've learned so much more about your . . . skills."

The smile faded from her lips, and she glanced back to the door to make sure nobody heard him. "This really isn't the place or time to discuss this, Matt."

"I don't want to make this awkward. I wanted to introduce you to someone who can help you—help us both—learn more about this."

About how I can hear and see the dead relive their last moments alive on this earth? All her life, Ryan thought her talent was merely amazing deduction. Then, to have Holbrook suggest that she might be a medium . . . that was information she wanted to keep between the two of them.

She turned toward him. "What we do is classified. We can't involve an outsider."

"She doesn't know what we do. I promise," Holbrook said, "but her insights could prove useful. To you, and me."

Ryan leaned back against the wall next to him and gazed up at the night sky. Amid the glow from the city lights, the stars barely glimmered against the dark backdrop. She sighed deeply and inched closer, resting her head against his shoulder. He tilted his head onto hers, and a warmth surged within her. This was their secret. She didn't want to share it with anyone else.

"I want to help you, Ryan," he said softly. "That's all I want."

She inhaled slowly. Matt understood that this was bigger than both of them. If this woman could help her, who was she to stand in the way? He only had the best intentions for SPECTER—and for her. He would never hurt her. Ever.

"Fine. I'll talk to her."

"Wonderful."

"But there can be absolutely no mention of SPECTER," she said, turning a pointed glance toward him.

"Agreed."

"And you'll be there the whole time?" Their faces were inches apart, and she could feel the warmth of his breath on her cheeks.

He nodded. "As long as you want me."

She tilted her head back toward the stars and wrapped her arms around herself, not merely against the faint chill in the air, but something deeper, something unknown. "Okay," she breathed.

"Tomorrow morning?" he asked and nudged her shoulder.

Ryan smiled. "Not too early."

"Alright." Matt nodded and stepped away from the wall, extending a hand to Ryan. "Shall we go back in? I need a shot of scotch."

"You're gonna be so hammered after tonight that you won't want to get up in the morning."

The open door filled the night air with loud music, a classic Southern rock song that everyone in the bar seemed to recognize.

"I'm not driving," he shouted over the music, "and another scotch will ensure that I definitely won't wake you up too early."

His accent sounded even more British than usual. He continued gripping Ryan's hand as he led her through the dance floor and toward the bar, where rows of TV screens flickered overhead.

As Holbrook ordered drinks, Ryan's gaze drifted to the TV screens. One flashed *Breaking News*—an Eastern family murdered, the eldest son in custody. The story hovered at the edge of her mind, then she shook her head. This wasn't her case. Not today.

She grasped the cold bottle of beer, its surface moist with condensation. The music's beat vibrated through the glass as she slid into the booth across from Holbrook. He launched into another story about something that had happened while she had been in Chicago. She held the bottle, enjoying the music and conversation. But never took a sip.

CHAPTER 3

The OverBoard ride-share car pulled up to the curb of Ryan's house. Before she could open the backseat door, Coti wrapped an arm around her shoulders and leaned in for a tight embrace, the odor of alcohol seeping from her pores.

"You know," Coti said, with eyes closed and head resting on Ryan's shoulder, "you're my best friend."

Ryan patted her cheek and grinned. Coti probably wouldn't remember any of this when she awoke with a hangover in the morning, but at least the sentiment was genuine.

"You saved my life and you'll always be my best friend," Coti said with a squeeze of her arm.

"You're my best friend, too," Ryan said, slowly slipping out from under the woman's arm.

Opening the door, she moved to step out when Holbrook reached across Coti's lap and grasped Ryan's wrist.

A silly grin spread across his face. "You know, you're *my* best friend, too."

"And you're drunk," she said, flashing a smile.

He erupted into laughter, and Coti giggled with him. Dave moaned from his drunken stupor in the front seat. Ryan pulled away from Holbrook. Before stepping out of the taxi, she spoke to the driver, who watched her from the rearview mirror.

"Please get them home safely," she said, slipping two twenty-dollar bills over the seat. She then stepped out of the car and closed the door. She watched the car drive away with Coti and Doc making silly faces out the back window.

They had too much fun tonight to even notice that Ryan didn't drink any alcohol. Just a bottled beverage that took on the appearance of beer but was nothing more than cream soda. Her smile fell away as she watched the car disappear beyond the streetlights. Now, she was alone with only her thoughts and the long night ahead of her.

The last of their voices still hummed in her head. *Best friend.* Coti had never called her that before. Probably the alcohol talking, but the girl had hugged her so tightly when she'd said it.

Ryan remembered her arms, clinging to her the night they'd been kidnapped. The night her former partner, Agent Sam Masters, had nearly cut Coti's throat before Ryan shot him. The night that triggered her own need for the therapy that would never work. Neither had spoken about what happened. But there were glances, a mutual respect for their shared horror. Perhaps that was enough to make them "best friends."

And then there was Matt and his silly, drunken grin. The memory of his goodbye made her smile. He always knew what to say to make her laugh. Maybe that was what she needed: the thought of him leaning across the back seat of the car, saying he was her friend too.

Once inside the house, Ryan activated the security system and turned on the lights throughout the first floor, banishing every shadow that lingered in the corners. The lights would remain on until morning, as they did every night. The six weeks she had spent at Quantico hadn't been enough to dispel the darkness. Not even the weapons training or the profiling program that Director Price had insisted that she take had helped. The dorms had been noisy, and the light streaming through the windows helped keep her mind occupied at night. But here it was different, and the thoughts crept back in once she was back in familiar surroundings.

Ryan padded up to the second floor, switching on every light until reaching her bedroom. Every muscle in her face ached from smiling and laughing all night. When she turned the bathroom light on, her throat tightened. The mirror. Immediately, the humor of the evening faded as she stood outside the bathroom, gazing at the upper edges of the mirror, to the facets that held it in place and the corners that curved downward toward the vanity.

Nothing but her reflection—like every night since that one when a serial killer invaded her space. No streaks of red forming words, no echoes of a sinister poem from her childhood. Nothing but her.

The man who wasn't there.

Ryan shivered. He was *always* there, lurking in the darkest shadows, waiting. But Sam, her former partner and a confessed murderer, was gone, having taken two bullets to the brain from her own gun and her own hand.

Since that horrific night, she hadn't been able to tolerate alcohol. The smell brought bad memories, and drinking it came with terrible nightmares of the way he smelled that night. It had sat on his breath and leaked from his pores, and every time he touched her, it sank into her skin. Going out with friends left her plenty sober to face these things on her own.

Shuddering, she turned away from the mirror and stepped back into the bedroom. The nightstand lamps flicked on with a touch of the main switch, yet they failed to expel any lingering demons. After changing into shorts and a tank top, Ryan slipped under the covers.

Like every night, she sat upright with the linens draped over her lap, staring into the lights surrounding her while listening to every sound from within the house. The ticking of the clock on the living room wall downstairs. The faint whoosh of air escaping the vents whenever the air conditioning kicked on. Every. Single. Sound. Until everything settled into a timed and predictable rhythm, and she was sure nobody had come up the stairs. It was after three in the morning by the time she opened the drawer of the nightstand. An orange prescription bottle label stared up at her.

Without it, she couldn't sleep. With it, she struggled to wake up in the morning, but at least she didn't have nightmares.

She tapped a single pill onto the palm of her hand. *Take away the dreams so I can get through another day.* She swallowed the capsule, then lay back against the pillow, the lamps burning bright as she closed her eyes.

****

Ryan slowly peeled open her eyes at the vibrating sound of the cell phone drilling into her ears. Sharp morning sunlight sliced through the blinds of the eastern-facing window. The effects of the pill still hovered over her like a cloud, but she managed to grasp the phone and peer at the screen.

I'll be there in about an hour.

The message was from Holbrook. Ryan squinted at his text. *Did we have plans today?* She sat up, and the world went into a tailspin. "Ohhh," she groaned and leaned back against her pillow.

She stared at the message, recalling the discussion in the back alley of the bar. Holbrook wanted her to meet someone. As drunk as everyone was last night, she was surprised that Matt was alive, let alone awake and planning to come over.

Swinging her legs over the side of the bed, Ryan slowly moved into a sitting position. This would require a lot of coffee, and she needed to get it into her system as fast as possible before Holbrook arrived. Struggling into a t-shirt and jeans, she tied back her long hair and shuffled slowly down the stairs to get the coffee pot started.

As it brewed, she turned on the television. Any background noise helped wake her up. Most of the stations played the same breaking news she noticed last night at the bar.

Wealthy family; all murdered in their beds; the oldest son arrested shortly after it had occurred. As she went to turn it off, her hand froze. Something tugged from the corner of her mind.

"Stop it, Ryan." The murder was in another county, out of her jurisdiction. Shaking her head, she snapped off the TV.

The heavy aroma of hot coffee filled the kitchen, and soon, the liquid, laced with sugar and cream, hit her stomach. Before the caffeine had a chance to take effect, a knock sounded at the door. Holbrook had wasted no time this morning.

Bright sunlight streamed through the open front door when she opened it. Doc stood on the porch with his usual grin, and this time, a woman stood beside him.

"Good morning," he said.

"Is it?" Ryan glanced from Holbrook to the woman. Taking a sip of coffee, she cringed as it hit the back of her throat.

"I certainly hope so." He turned toward the woman, who offered a gentle smile. She appeared ten to fifteen years older than Ryan, but it barely showed, except for the faint lines around her mouth and eyes. Full auburn hair framed an oval face and gently cascaded over the woman's shoulders.

Holbrook lightly placed a hand on the woman's shoulder. "Ryan, I'd like you to meet Summer. Summer, this is Ryan Mills."

"Summer." Ryan was waiting for a last name, but when none was offered, she simply nodded and stepped aside. "Come in, please."

"Doc mentioned you were coming," Ryan said as she removed the unfolded blanket from the couch. "I had a late start this morning. Sorry the place isn't very tidy." There really wasn't much out of place in the living room, though. She'd spent little time at home over the last several months, especially after Director Price insisted she go to Quantico for six weeks of training. Then there was the Stephen Jeffries case.

Holbrook and Summer sat on the couch while Ryan pulled an oak chair from the dining room table and sat opposite them.

"We had a late night together," Holbrook said with a laugh.

"Well," Ryan interrupted, setting her mug on the coffee table, "not *together*, together. It was an . . . office thing. A party, so to speak."

Summer smiled and flashed a glance at Holbrook.

"Right," he said, cheeks flushing. "Summer's been a good friend of mine for a long time, and I thought it was time you two met, especially given your current circumstance."

"My *circumstance?*" Ryan said, sitting up a little straighter, her head tilting to one side as she kept her eyes on Matt.

"Um—" Holbrook started, but Summer placed a hand on his forearm.

"I've got this," she interjected. Holbrook exhaled a nervous, relieved sigh. "Matt has told me about you, and we agreed that I might be able to help you in some way."

Ryan raised an eyebrow and glanced toward Holbrook, her lips tightly pressed together. "How much *did* he tell you?"

Summer continued, her even-toned, unflustered gaze exuding quiet confidence. "I know you both work together in law enforcement, but he also mentioned that much of it is classified.

However, that's not why I'm here," she said softly, shaking her head. "You see, Ryan, I'm a medium."

The floor almost dropped from under Ryan's feet. *How much had Holbrook told her?* This was a secret, something they discovered in the last year, and nobody outside of the lab knew about it. The word *medium* had only recently become part of her vocabulary, a term she barely accepted and still wasn't sure she was ready to fully embrace.

She shot a cold and pointed gaze at Holbrook. His face turned pale, and his usual smile vanished.

"I sort of figured it out, really," Summer said, a knowing smile gracing her lips. "It's what I do."

Ryan slid her hands between her crossed legs. The last thing she wanted was to show her nervousness by chomping on the tips of her nails in front of a stranger.

"I'm sorry if I've made you uncomfortable." Summer leaned forward. "But I'm here for a reason. This 'condition' isn't a disease, but it can be challenging to navigate. That's why I'm here—to mentor you. Matt mentioned some of the things you've done, and I've got to say that I'm impressed."

"So you *did* tell her?" she said, her gaze fixed on Holbrook's shrinking form.

Summer leaned back, forming a steeple with her fingers as they rested against her lips. Several tense moments passed. "You're a very powerful medium," she said slowly. "It's something you've had all your life. Did either of your parents have the gift?"

A hollow pit formed inside her stomach, and Ryan's eyes dropped to the ground. "I don't know," she murmured as a silence fell over the room.

"They died in a car accident when you were very young," Summer said.

"How did you know that?" Ryan stammered.

"Your aura," Summer explained. "It changed when I asked about your parents. It could only mean tragedy—I sensed a deep pain that's been with you for a long time."

Ryan swallowed the lump forming in her throat. She didn't want this. Holbrook had no right to do this to her. "Thank you, but I really don't see how you can help me."

"I know you've experienced deep loss in your life—not only your parents. It's been a dark cloud following you that has recently lifted."

"I never told her anything about that," Holbrook interjected quickly, as though he could read Ryan's thoughts.

He *must* have hinted about her sister, Lexi, and the case that brought her to SPECTER in the first place.

"Perhaps, Matt, you can leave us alone for a few moments?" Summer asked.

Holbrook nodded. "I'll be outside if you need me."

After the click of the door shutting, Ryan leaned forward. "Listen. I don't know you, and I don't need your help. And Holbrook had no right to spring this on me. I'm not a sideshow for exploitation, nor will I be your apprentice." Her heart pounded in her chest. Yet, despite her angry declarations, something deep inside told her that this woman would be part of her life, somehow.

"Matt didn't tell me anything," Summer continued. "He didn't have to. This loss . . . a sibling. So many years ago. But you found her. You had closure, though it came at a painful cost."

Ryan turned toward her. "Tell me something that Matt doesn't know. So far, you've only spouted information that almost anyone who knows me could provide."

"This thing that left a wound that won't heal—it follows

you. You keep lights on to chase the shadows, yet still, it won't let you sleep."

Ryan inhaled sharply, forcing herself to keep breathing. She had never told anyone about the nightmares or the insomnia—about the shadows that tormented her and the stain of the one who'd deeply scarred her. Her fingers clutched the arms of the chair in white-knuckle grips as she slipped back into it.

"The memory of it . . . haunts you." Rising, Summer paced the room with her arms folded across her chest, then paused at the base of the stairs. "He was here," she breathed, gazing up toward the shadowed second-floor landing. "He defiled this place, and it makes you afraid."

Ryan couldn't bring herself to look at her. Unable to release her grip, she heard nothing but the pounding of her own blood and Summer's steady voice.

The woman placed one finger on the banister, then inhaled sharply, jumping back, her eyes widening. "A man . . . a man who wasn't there," she said.

Ryan bit her lip, and blood trickled into her mouth. With joints stiff and each movement laced with pain, she leaped up as Summer turned to face her. Ryan met the medium's gaze as though she'd known this woman since childhood. Ryan knew that there was no secret this woman couldn't uncover.

In a hushed, synchronized murmur, their voices recited the familiar refrain—a poem known by heart, yet one Ryan wished she could forget:

"He wasn't there again today."

CHAPTER 4

Ryan made tea, and Summer motioned for them to sit at the dining room table.

"Should we get Holbrook?" Ryan asked.

"Not yet," Summer replied, taking a sip. She placed her cup on the tray, then met Ryan's eyes. "The one who did this to you, he still haunts you every day," she whispered.

"Yes," Ryan muttered.

"You're afraid that if you can see others who have died violently, then someday you'll see him."

Ryan's mouth went dry, but she forced a response. "Yes." She still felt the brush of Stephen Jefferies' breath on the back of her neck in the forest clearing, as though he still stood behind her. What if Sam waited in the darkest corners of the house for her as well?

Summer inhaled and took Ryan's hands in hers. "You need to learn how to shield yourself. I can't guarantee you'll never see him, but I can help you now if you do."

That's not what Ryan wanted to hear. She needed reassurance. That she was merely spiraling into post-traumatic stress again. All those mandatory sessions with the FBI-issued psychologist, after she was kidnapped and forced to shoot her partner, did little to calm her fears. She needed Summer to tell her it was all in her head and that things would get better.

But that's not what the medium said.

Summer placed her hands on the table. "When they come to you, how does it happen?"

"I used to think it was my imagination conjuring scenarios of the murder. I even gave them names," Ryan admitted.

"And you were right about the names most of the time, weren't you?"

Ryan nodded. "I can see them before the murder. One minute they are here and then . . . I hear them, though I used to think I was my imagination. And sometimes, I can feel their pain when they died."

"Ah, clairaudience and clairsentience. Very interesting." Summer nodded. "I knew you were powerful." She pulled back her long shirt sleeves to her elbows. "First, what you need to practice is shielding, at least until we can work on other techniques."

"Shielding?"

"It's a way to psychically protect yourself. Some of these presences can be rather . . . forceful when they want to be. Have you ever channeled one of them?"

Ryan wasn't sure what Summer meant, but she flashed back to the last moments before she shot Sam—when every one of his victims stirred within the darkest corners of the underground cellar where he had held her captive. They had surrounded her, each stepping into her mind and compelling her to stand when she had nothing left. Because of them, she'd managed to catch Sam off guard long enough to grab her weapon.

An acrid scent of gunpowder filled her nostrils as the memory of Sam's head jerking back when the bullets struck his forehead raced through her mind, leaving her throat tight.

"I sense that you *have* channeled them," Summer whispered, reaching across the table to touch Ryan's arm.

"I didn't do it on purpose. I don't know how it happened."

"They entered you," Summer said gently. "It wasn't your choice."

"But they saved me," Ryan insisted. "He would have killed me if they hadn't intervened."

"I believe you, but they can also do it against your will, and it may not be for your benefit."

The thought of another entity using her body like a puppet made her chest tighten.

"And others may continue to seek your attention long after you're done with them. Think of them as persistent children who tug at your shirt sleeves and don't know when to stop. Sometimes, you have to say, 'Enough is enough.' That's where shielding comes in."

"I understand," Ryan said, shifting uncomfortably, attempting to suppress her doubts and later disappointment. She already saw the dead, so perhaps learning how to control them would equate to controlling Sam's unwanted intrusions. "Okay. Where do I start?"

"This won't be as easy as it sounds," Summer warned. "In a calm environment like this, you can *practice* shielding, but once you're under attack, everything changes. They will bombard your senses and scatter your thoughts, using every tactic available to disrupt your concentration. You *must* remain calm, maintain your focus. You can't let them undermine your control. Focus is your weapon. Do you understand?"

Summer's unyielding gaze fixed on Ryan, who was starting to feel the full weight of the challenge. It wouldn't be easy, but she had no other choice. She nodded.

"Good. First, you need to ground yourself. To do this, use your five senses until your mind is focused. Close your eyes. Now, imagine a wall surrounding you, built with whatever materials you choose."

Ryan listened, but a nagging concern burrowed into her thoughts. How could mere imagination protect her from the unseen? None of the presences had ever tried to injure her—they only sought the peace and justice she offered. Yet, the idea that something might deliberately try to harm her sent shivers crawling down her arms like spiders.

Summer's voice floated in Ryan's mind. "Concentrate on maintaining that wall against all forms of attack. Do you have your wall?"

Ryan tried to imagine a sturdy stone wall, and she was the center. The minerals became translucent, as if like glass. "I think so. I guess I don't have the right kind of imagination."

Summer inhaled. "Perhaps this will help. If something keeps charging at you, and it will, yell at it. Tell it to go away. You have power in your voice. *You* command the scene. Think of it like an obnoxious guy at the bar who won't take the hint."

Ryan smirked as she opened her eyes. "Walls. Say no. Got it."

Summer reached into her pocket and withdrew a card, but before Ryan could accept it, her cell phone rang. She glanced down at the screen: Director Price.

"I'm sorry," Ryan said as she stood. "I've got to take this."

She stepped away from the table and opened the front door, where Holbrook was sitting on the porch, reading a newspaper. She waved him back into the house.

"Hello," she said, mouthing the words 'Director Price' toward Matt, who nodded.

"Are you home right now?"

"Yes, sir."

"Have you been watching the news?"

Her brow furrowed as she exchanged a quick, puzzled glance at Holbrook, who silently shrugged a big *what.* "No, but I can turn it on." Grabbing the remote from the coffee table, she switched on the television to the same channel broadcasting the breaking news she had ignored earlier.

Sure enough, the same grim story dominated the screen: the high-profile murder and the case of the eldest son now charged with the crime.

"I've got it on now," she said. "You mean the murder?"

"I need you and the team out there to assist the investigation tonight. There's a jet waiting at the airport, departing at seventeen hundred today," Price instructed.

"Assist? Sir, I don't understand—this is a murder case where a suspect is already in custody. Why do you need us?"

Price's tone sharpened. "I'm sending you a file on the case. Check your inbox in about five minutes. This is top priority."

Ryan's brow furrowed as her confusion deepened. She glanced at Holbrook, who stopped his attempts at probing for details.

"I understand, sir. We'll be at the airport and ready to leave at seventeen hundred," she confirmed. Then the line went dead.

Holbrook's expression mirrored her own. As he stepped away, she slowly lowered the phone as the news broadcast continued to loop the shaky, semi-blurred footage of the suspect being cuffed and loaded into a patrol car. At the bottom of the screen, a scrolling headline read: *Tech innovator J.J. Harrison and family found slain in Vermont home. 19-year-old son in custody.*

"What is it?" Holbrook said.

As the video of the son's arrest replayed, Ryan turned toward Holbrook. "We're going to Vermont. Tonight."

CHAPTER 5

Ryan and her team didn't have much time to shake off their hangovers, let alone pack the needed equipment for the trip. The Lazarus room remained silent as each case was filled with cords, power strips, lights, and every component of the mini-Lazarus system. However, this time was different. They were headed to an active crime scene farther than the team had ever travelled—a clear sign that Director Price had faith in them.

But this case was urgent. As Ryan read Price's email, her chest tightened, and even the vast airport hangar wasn't enough room to help her breathe as they waited for the private jet. Her fingers gripped the handle of the briefcase containing a printed case file for each member of SPECTER.

What lingered most were Summer's parting words before she and Holbrook headed to the lab: "I sense a great evil. One you are not ready to face, but face it you must."

Ryan silently wished for a last-minute delay. Yet, deep down, she knew that would only postpone the inevitable, and she sensed they were heading toward something far different from anything they'd faced before.

A warm breeze danced through the open hangar bay as they waited, surrounded by neatly arranged crates of equipment. A single jet taxied along the distant runway, catching the late-day sunlight in a blinding gleam of white along its fuselage. Ryan's uneasiness continued to swarm in her gut as the plane steadily approached the private terminal like a slow-moving bullet.

She turned when she felt a gentle nudge on her shoulder. A hand-length taller, Holbrook stood at her side, his heavy brow casting a soft shadow over his warm brown eyes.

"You seem troubled," he whispered.

She drew in a steady, purposeful breath, choosing her words with care. "I guess I am."

"It's this case, isn't it? Are we getting any information on it inflight?"

"Yes," she replied with a nod. "Director Price has labeled this as extremely confidential. I'm sorry, but I'm not allowed to discuss it until we are airborne."

"I understand, but I've never seen you this jittery about a case before. This one must be a banger."

"It is," Ryan said as the plane entered the hangar. This case made her insides crawl, not because of the pressure to prove themselves to Price, but because of the chilling crime scene photos that left her cold. She had encountered countless similar situations, yet this time, an indescribable disquiet settled deep within her soul. As much as she would love to showcase her team's skills in solving this case, she sensed they should avoid it at all costs.

She turned to Matt, who frowned slightly at the worry in her eyes. He placed a reassuring hand on her shoulder. "I'm here for you, Ryan. Always."

Ryan boarded the plane in silence, the weight of what lay ahead pressing on her. Another case. Another family torn apart. Another child missing. They knew who pulled the trigger—but not why. And where was the youngest child? Did she meet the same fate as her family?

"Whoa!" Coti exclaimed as she slipped past Ryan. "Check out the digs."

The FBI had arranged some impressive amenities: wide leather seats lined the cabin walls, accented by square windows. Instead of the typical hard rubber walkways, a plush blue wall-to-wall carpet covered the floor, bathed in the glow of overhead lights. And, she'd been informed, with the push of a button, a table would unfold from the floor, creating a workspace for the team's briefing.

Outside, crewmen loaded the luggage and equipment cases into the cargo bay under Holbrook's supervision. He personally ensured every container was locked down and secure. Then, once the gear was stowed, the rest of the team filed in and settled into their seats.

A female flight attendant in a pressed, navy-blue pantsuit approached. "Can I get you anything to drink before we take off, Special Agent Mills? We have champagne, wine—"

A catch started in Ryan's throat. Of course, the woman knew her name. This was the FBI. "Um, water, please." The woman nodded and then moved on to the other passengers.

A few minutes later, Holbrook settled into the seat next to her. As he clipped the seatbelt around his lap, the attendant asked for Matt's refreshment order. "May I have an English Breakfast tea, loose leaf, with one sugar, please?" he asked.

The attendant smiled and nodded. "Of course, sir."

Ryan clutched the briefcase resting on her lap. The documents inside shifted very little, but with the slight movement of the plane as the team boarded, it felt like they were trying to crawl and claw their way to escape. Each one of those horrid photographs slithered inside the case beneath her hand.

The captain's voice echoed through the PA system as the

door slammed shut. Ryan closed her eyes, and Holbrook's hand covered hers where it rested on the case. The captain spoke, but she barely heard his words as she glanced at Holbrook, who gave her a knowing nod.

He couldn't know—not yet. He had no idea what they were getting into. Ryan clutched the briefcase tighter.

As the jet leveled off at cruising altitude, all eyes shifted to Ryan. After the table rose from the floor, everyone sidled closer.

"So, what's with all the secrecy?" Coti asked, shattering the uneasy silence. "Did some senator get whacked or something?"

"Or something," Ryan muttered as she unclasped her briefcase and distributed a sealed goldenrod envelope to each team member before taking out her laptop.

"I wasn't allowed to divulge any information until we were inflight," Ryan explained, powering up her computer. Opening the digital file Director Price sent earlier that morning, she nodded to the group.

"Please open your files," Ryan instructed.

Dave glanced at Coti and Doc, who shared similarly quizzical expressions, before opening their packages.

"Our destination is Currant Falls, Vermont, where an FBI team already on the scene will meet us."

"Wait," Dave interrupted, peering above the rim of his glasses. "Currant Falls, Vermont? You mean we're going to—"

"Yes."

Coti shook her head, her gaze shifting between them. "I'm lost. What the hell is in Vermont?"

Dave swallowed hard. "We've been called to assist on the J.J. Harrison investigation, right?"

"Correct."

Holbrook scanned the documents. "I see," he exhaled.

Coti's eyes widened. "Are you serious?"

"I'm afraid so," Ryan replied, looking at the file open on her laptop. "As you know, J.J. Harrison, the multi-billionaire creator of the SmilePage social media platform, was murdered last night, along with his wife and two youngest sons. The oldest son, Chad, who is nineteen, has been arrested for the murders."

A heavy silence had fallen as Ryan spoke. Photographs spilled out from the folders, showcasing dozens of blood-stained carpets and furniture, as well as the bodies of the family members.

"My god, this is horrible," Coti muttered, her hand flying to her lips.

Holbrook sighed and pushed the photos beneath the stack of other documents. "I'm curious. Did Director Price mention why we were called to assist? This doesn't seem like our jurisdiction. A murder was committed, and the suspect has been caught. Do they suspect that perhaps the son wasn't the killer?"

Ryan shook her head, her mouth suddenly dry. She had entertained the same doubts until reading the next part of the file. "The son confessed to the murders. In fact, he called the police himself, then sat on the front step and waited for them."

"Then I don't get it," Dave said, his brow furrowed. "What do they need us for? Looks like an open-and-shut case."

"Not quite." Ryan cleared her throat, taking a moment to gather her thoughts. "Harrison had four children: his oldest son, Chad, two younger sons, aged fourteen and twelve, and . . . a five-year-old daughter."

"Wait," Coti spoke. "What happened to the girl? She's not in any of these photos."

"Exactly. She's the reason we're here." Ryan turned her computer toward the team and displayed the photograph of a young child, her widest and most beautiful smile lighting up the screen.

Her blonde hair, perfectly curled, no doubt by her mother, gleamed in the photographer's flash. "This is five-year-old Emma Harrison. She's missing, and the suspect isn't talking. The FBI team on-site hasn't found any leads to locate her."

Ryan leaned forward, scanning the faces of her team. "It's been over twenty-four hours since the murders, and the weather hasn't cooperated. Night temperatures are dropping, and we're running out of time. Director Price thinks we could uncover hidden clues that might help locate her—either the girl or her body."

"Wait a moment," Holbrook said, leaning his elbows on the table. "We've never done anything like this before. We deal in dead energy imprinted on the environment. Not the living."

"I understand," Ryan said, turning her computer back to face the screen. "But Director Price believes our unique skill set could help."

"How?" Dave said. "Unless she's dead . . . and god-willing, she's not . . . how in the world are we supposed to find her?"

Ryan clasped her fingers together and leaned back in the chair. "By talking to those who were there the night she went missing."

Silence fell over the group again.

Holbrook nodded. "Perhaps," he said slowly, "we can see all angles of the crime in the very place it happened."

"Directly from the Harrison family," Dave whispered.

"Someone must have seen what happened that night," Ryan said. "They might know whether Chad killed her and where he put her if he did, or if she managed to escape. There might be a memory imprinted on the environment that could give us a clue."

A faint smile appeared on Holbrook's lips. "I believe Director Price was correct. We may be able to help after all."

CHAPTER 6

The sky had darkened by the time the plane landed, and rain pelted the metal hull as it taxied toward the private hangar. Ryan slipped on her suit coat over her crisp, white, button-down shirt and smoothed down the collar. She at least looked the part of an FBI agent, even if she was about to get drenched.

A rumble of thunder vibrated along the tarmac as Ryan descended the plane's steps. She hurried into the shelter of the private hangar, which was much smaller than the one they'd departed from, as was the rest of the airport.

"Special Agent Mills?" a voice called out. A man in a fitted suit and tie, short-cropped hair, and broad shoulders approached with an outstretched hand.

She shook his hand. "Yes."

"I'm Agent James Brooks. I'm here to take you to the sheriff's department."

"Alright," she said and glanced back to Holbrook and Coti, who were entering the hangar. "My team will be ready as soon as they unload."

"Another car will take them and your equipment to the hotel. My orders are to bring only you, Agent Mills. It's urgent."

Her grip tightened on the briefcase handle. "Okay. I'll inform my team."

She turned away before he could protest and met Holbrook

at the edge of the hangar. His thick hair dripped with water, and he did his best to brush it out of his eyes.

"They are taking me to the station," she said. "They'll take you to the hotel and I'll meet you there."

She started to step away, but Holbrook stopped her. "Wait one moment." He reached into his jacket pocket and withdrew a watch with a smooth, black face, identical to the demo piece he'd shown her at the lab. "Here. I managed to make a few final adjustments before we left. I'd like you to try it out during the investigation. Maybe even now."

"Perfect." She took the watch and strapped it on. "I'll see you when I'm finished." She nodded and headed back toward the waiting agent.

The downpour muffled the last traces of the jet engines as Ryan stepped into the SUV with Agent Brooks. He pulled away from the small airport and onto the dark, winding roads of Vermont, a state she had never visited. Between the relentless rain and the pitch-black skies, she saw little of the landscape, aside from the dense walls of deep green trees flanking the road. There could have been miles of forest beyond that, but the rain-streaked windows concealed the view.

The road opened at the edge of a town. Small storefronts with darkened windows and 'Closed' placards flashed past in brief glimpses. There were very few traffic lights, most simply flashing an orange light due to the hour.

Even in the storm, the glow of lights and cars created a beacon marking their destination. The local police station parking lot was packed with vehicles and news vans with transmitters jutting from their roofs. The rain didn't deter the crowd of reporters standing outside the building—too many reporters for a town this small. No doubt national broadcasters drawn by the magnitude of the story.

"We are not releasing any information to the press at this time," Brooks said. The SUV rocked slightly as they eased into the lot, the throng of reporters parting to let them through. "And don't speak to them either," he said, nodding toward the crowd.

Before the car came to a complete stop, reporters swarmed the SUV like parasites attacking a fresh host. Hands pounded on the windows as overlapping voices shouted questions, demanding interviews.

As rain fell in heavy splatters on the windshield, Brooks unbuckled his seatbelt and glanced at her. "Ready?"

"As ready as I'll ever be."

Ryan stepped from the vehicle and into chaos. Men and women thrust digital recorders and microphones toward her face. The multitude of voices merged with the rain, forming a single deafening roar. She attempted to push through the wall of arms that were trying to block or grab her until a firm grip landed on her shoulder. Brooks bulldozed through the crowd, clearing a path to the entrance of the police department.

As the double glass doors closed behind them, the noise faded to a murmur. At least the press wasn't allowed inside, which made the walk through the lobby blessedly quiet. Brooks led her down the left hallway past a corridor of offices. Wall-mounted signs pointed toward the main office, the records department, and their destination—the jail and interrogation rooms.

The agent slowed, gesturing toward a pair of closed doors with narrow window panels revealing a group of men seated around a long table. Brooks pushed open the doors and allowed her into the conference room.

As Ryan stepped inside, a half-dozen heads turned in her

direction. A few of the men stood, a holdover from old tradition, and these men were old enough to remember it. The man closest to the doors swiveled in his chair. His dark, neatly styled hair held a slight brush of grey at the temples, and the black, tailored suit and tie clearly marked him as one of the FBI agents on the case.

Brooks stopped at the end of the table and glanced at the men. "This is Special Agent Mills."

"Agent," the man in the swivel chair said, finally standing. His tall, lean frame and muscled shoulders curved under the fitted suit jacket. He smiled—an expression that appeared a little coy, even if it wasn't meant to be. "I'm Agent James Finn. Welcome to Vermont." He held out his hand.

She shook it, his grasp firm and arm rigid, as if testing her strength. "Agent Finn," she replied.

He released her hand and turned to the rest of the group. The man standing to Finn's left appeared to be about her age and not much taller. His brown, long-sleeved button-down shirt bore a silver badge, and a cluster of emblems over the chest told her everything she needed to know about him.

"This is Sheriff Watson," Agent Finn said.

The man's soft hazel eyes creased at the corners as he offered a smile beneath a well-trimmed goatee. "You can call me Cole."

She shook his steady hand, which lacked the ferocity of Finn's grip test.

Finn went on to introduce her to the others: a mix of agents, deputies, and even the mayor. All of them were now deeply involved in a case that had turned their small town into the center of a nationwide, high-profile mass murder investigation.

"Have you been fully briefed?" Finn asked.

Ryan nodded. "Director Price has updated me."

She noticed an almost imperceptible frown cross his face.

"May we talk for a moment?" His green-grey eyes tightened with that same thin smile. He nodded toward the door and followed her into the hallway.

Out of the view of the others, his tall frame leaned forward slightly, hands resting on his hips. She didn't need to look to know the smile had vanished the moment they were alone.

"Director Price," Finn said, his voice laced with sarcasm. "I'm curious. How is it I've never heard of Price until today?"

Ryan's jaw tightened as she clutched the briefcase. "That's not my problem. I was sent here to assist, nothing more. My team isn't taking over the investigation."

"We don't need your help."

The moment the thought entered her brain, she knew saying it would be venomous, but she couldn't stop herself.

"Then where is Emma Harrison?"

His nostrils flared, and his arms instantly crossed over his broad chest. He let out a careful breath, eyes locked on her. "I've never heard of the SPECTER division. What is it?"

"It's classified," she shot back, stepping an inch closer, straightening her spine. There was no way to match his height or swimmer's build, but she wasn't about to get bullied by another agent.

"I have clearance." Again, the coy smile tickled the edges of his mouth despite his arms remaining crossed.

"Not this high, you don't."

The smile slipped, as did the faint creases at the corners of his eyes. Something behind them cooled, recalculated. "Very well," he said tightly. "How can you *assist* my team?"

Her voice lowered. This part might have been classified even beyond what the sheriff or mayor was cleared to hear. "We need access to the crime scene—and exactly as you found it."

"The bodies have already been taken to the morgue, and the CSI team is on-site collecting evidence."

"That's fine. Leave it the way it is once they're done. Don't let the clean-up crew in yet."

His brow furrowed, and his arms dropped to his sides. "What exactly can you do that the CSI can't?"

Now it was her time to be coy. She leaned in, tipping her head enough to signal discretion. He understood the gesture, bending forward to hear the secret she had implied.

A steady breath slipped past her lips, now mere inches from his ear. At this distance, she could smell the faint trace of after-shave on his neck and see the slightest shadow of stubble on his skin.

"It's classified," she whispered.

Finn straightened at once, shooting her a sideways glance with one raised eyebrow. "Fine." He looked into the conference room where the others waited for Ryan to speak. Then he turned back to her. "I can get you in there at first light tomorrow."

"That could be too late. Emma is still out there somewhere, and maybe there's a chance she's still alive."

He held up a hand in surrender. "I understand, but the storm has hampered the investigation. It's dangerous to head out there right now, and my team is still searching the grounds. The CSI team will be done gathering evidence inside the house tonight. By morning, I can give you full access with no one to disturb your people. Okay?"

Ryan hadn't flown out here with her team on short notice only to be told they had to wait. That wasn't good enough, but she also had to work with the crime scene techs. As a former police detective, she hated it when someone wanted to disturb her scene before she had finished her sweep. She fully understood Finn's position of control.

And maybe, just maybe, Finn's team would find the missing girl before dawn. She listened to the rain pounding on the station roof.

"Okay," she said with a sigh.

"In the meantime," Finn said, his voice dropping, "I could probably use your help." He turned his back toward the conference room doors, only speaking loud enough for her to hear. "We have Chad Harrison here, and he's not talking. I've tried interviewing him—"

Ryan's fingertips went numb, and the nervous swarm of unruly bees stirred in her gut again. "Wait. He's still here?"

He nodded. "No one's been able to get anything from him since he was brought in."

The same tingling sensation she'd felt before boarding the plane crept back into her arms and legs. "But . . . I thought he confessed."

"Well, the only time he's spoken was during the 911 call—and yes, he did confess over the phone. But he hasn't said a word since. Maybe he'll talk to you. We've got to try, because we think he knows where the girl is."

She had interviewed hundreds of suspects before—many of them as guilty as she'd known them to be. In the early days, interrogations made her anxious. She didn't want to screw it up and look bad in front of her partner or mess up the case. But this case was unusual, and she wasn't sure why.

The more she reviewed the file, the more she wanted to crawl into a hole and shut her eyes. Still, if there was even the slightest hope that he knew something, she had to try.

"Alright," she said with a nod. "Let's see what Harrison has to tell us."

CHAPTER 7

Ryan waited in the observation area. Harsh fluorescent light washed over the empty interrogation room's bland, windowless walls, visible through the one-way mirror.

The two men beside her said nothing, their nervous energy compounding her own. On her right, Sheriff Watson, Cole, if she remembered correctly, swayed slightly on his feet, probably didn't know he was even doing it. Finn, stoically on her left, remained as still as a statue, square jaw set, eyes narrowed in anticipation.

She fought the urge to bite her nails. Most of those bad habits had been conditioned out of her at Quantico. But today, even her tactical focus felt shaken, and the old impulses threatened to return with a vengeance.

The door to the interrogation room opened. That sudden motion made Ryan's stomach drop, and her hands clench into fists at her sides.

A young man in matching dark grey, jail-issued clothes stepped into the room, silver handcuffs fastened at his waist. *Chad Harrison.* A jolt through her nerves, and she shifted her weight.

A deputy guided him by the arm toward the table. The boy seemed unaware of his surroundings. There was something disturbingly vacant in the way he moved—like he was half there or waiting for someone to arrive. He slumped into the chair, his dark brown hair falling over shadowed eyes, his shoulders sagging as he stared blankly at the tabletop.

The deputy took his place against the wall, close enough to intervene if the suspect turned violent.

"Well," Finn said, turning to a digital control panel and activating the recording mechanism. "There's Chad Harrison, in the flesh."

He flashed a half-smile, but it wasn't the same coy expression from earlier. The whites of his eyes had grown paler, and the tension in his neck flexed beneath his white shirt collar.

"Are you ready?" he asked her.

There was no way to answer that truthfully. "As ready as I'll ever be."

"Okay. I'll go in first, wait a minute, then you follow."

Standing this close to Chad Harrison left her colder than she'd felt since entering the station. The boy sat in the chair like an empty lump of clay, unmoving, unblinking, but she couldn't take her eyes off him. The stiller he became, the stronger her instinct to back away, which was something she'd never felt during an interrogation, not even with the worst offenders.

Everything about Chad Harrison screamed terrible things that she couldn't hear but felt in her chest. Heavy, unreadable. She couldn't name it, but it was there. Waiting.

There had been hundreds of killers like this during her career, and they'd never looked the way you'd expect—evil incarnate, with a swastika carved into their foreheads like Charles Manson. Most looked like the guy next door. An ordinary man you'd pass on the street without a second glance.

Like Chad Harrison. The nineteen-year-old kid slouched in his chair with a mop of dark hair and a scruff of facial hair that hadn't yet grown to its full adult potential. Yet, there was something about him that made the hair on Ryan's arms rise as she watched him through the glass.

"Good luck," Colter Watson said.

Ryan jumped and glanced at him, his pupils dilated from the dim light in the room. Or . . . maybe he sensed something, too.

"Thanks, Cole." She turned her attention back to the suspect.

"You'll need it. I don't think he's gonna talk to you." His gaze stayed fixed on the boy. "I've known Chad and his family for years, and I've never seen him like this. I can't imagine him doing this."

Watson spoke as if to someone else in the room, not necessarily to her, but to the space around them. He continued swaying gently from side to side, one hand playing with the facial hair on his chin.

Ryan didn't know how to respond, so she only nodded. Most of the murderers she'd interrogated were first-time offenders, and their family and friends never saw it coming. There was no way to console them afterward.

Whatever made a man snap, it happened in every one of those cases—stress, depression, anxiety. There was always a trigger. Something that tipped the balance. This case was no different. Given enough time, the sheriff would see it, too.

When Finn entered the interrogation room, the swarms in Ryan's stomach whorled tighter. The agent's voice came through the observation room's speakers, every word clear and concise.

"Hi, Chad," he started. "I think you remember me. I'm Agent Finn with the FBI."

The boy didn't respond. He didn't even blink. He continued to stare at the bare tabletop, shoulders drooping as if whatever made him *him* wasn't inside the body anymore.

Ryan swallowed against the dryness in her throat, her eyes

dropping to the watch on her wrist. Pressing the on button, the screen activated, ready to notify her of any electromagnetic disturbances. *Might as well start the investigation now, and not only with interrogation techniques.* Holbrook gave her the device to test—this was the perfect time to start.

"I brought someone with me tonight," Finn said, flashing a glance toward the one-way mirror. That was her cue. She took a deep breath, sharp and quick, then stepped out of the observation room.

She took a deep breath, sharp and quick, then stepped out of the observation room. A chill brushed against the bare skin of her hands, and her legs faltered for a moment when she gazed at Chad Harrison.

No one-way mirror to separate them now.

She took the seat beside Agent Finn, directly across from the suspect.

"Hello, Chad," she started, keeping her voice even. "I'm Special Agent Mills."

The boy didn't move. No flicker of acknowledgement. He sat like someone in a half-drugged state. Through the curtain of dark hair, she caught a glimpse of vacant brown eyes—unfocused, unmoving.

Resting her hands on her lap, Ryan glanced at her watch. The black screen remained quiet. No movement. No signal. No abnormal electromagnetic signals. Good. Still, that didn't explain the surge of anxiety erupting inside her. Why did this interrogation make her nervous?

She looked up at the boy, and the only sound was the steady rhythm of breath escaping his nostrils.

"Can I get you anything, Chad?" she started. "Water? Food?"

Nothing. No emotion, no twitch. Not even an eye blink.

"I'd like to ask you a few questions, if that's okay." She sat up straighter and tilted her head to get a better look at his face. "Chad?" she said softly. "Do you remember what happened last night, before you called the police?"

Silence.

"Do you remember shooting your parents in the head with a rifle?" Agent Finn interrupted, his voice rising as he leaned on the table.

Ryan placed a firm hand on the agent's shoulder. If he wanted her help, he'd have to trust her lead, and this wasn't the way to do it. An angry approach would only make this kid retreat further. She furrowed her brow when Finn glanced at her, and, after a beat, he eased back in his chair.

"Chad," she said. "I know you're in shock. I'm here to help you in any way that I can."

Neither Finn's aggression nor her calm elicited a response. But Ryan had just started. She wasn't giving up that easily. She needed a different approach. The only other information she'd received was from Sheriff Watson.

"I know something about you, Chad." This time, she rested her hands on the table and leaned in, keeping her jaw loose, her expression soft as she caught his eye. "You loved your family. You didn't want to hurt them . . . did you?"

Chad's eyes flashed up—for a second.

Ryan's breath caught.

A faint vibration buzzed at her wrist, drawing her attention. She glanced down to see a series of green dots pointing in front of her. Pointing at Chad Harrison.

When she looked back up, his gaze had dropped again— back to the table, blank and distant.

I struck a nerve. He's in there, somewhere.

Ryan drew in a slow breath. "That's true, isn't it, Chad?" She held back the urge to ask more questions. "You didn't want this to happen. And you loved your little sister."

The watch vibrated again. This time with persistent, insistent pulses.

She didn't dare look down. If he moved, even slightly, she needed to see it.

"You loved Emma, didn't you?"

The vibrations grew stronger, nearly rattling against the surface of the table.

"Where is Emma? What did you do with her?"

Chad's head jerked—like an involuntary spasm had seized his neck. His eyes snapped up to hers, but were no longer brown. A black void stared at her, and within the darkness, a single flash of silver light glowed, like an animal caught in the dark.

The watch buzzed furiously now, drilling into the skin of her wrist. Ryan instinctively pulled her hands back from the table.

A faint smile curled up at the sides of Chad's pale, cracked lips.

"Where is she?" Ryan said again, her voice rising.

The twitch in Chad's neck happened again, sharp, sudden. Then his head dropped, his face went slack, and his hair fell forward, masking his eyes like a discarded marionette.

"Chad?" Ryan tilted her head to see his eyes.

Soft brown. The smile was gone. He was empty again.

The vibrations in her watch ceased, leaving only ghostly remnants in her nerves.

She eased back in the chair, eyes fixed on him. There was nothing more to get from Chad Harrison. *He isn't here anymore.*

As she studied the boy, her thoughts tracked through her mind, like they did at any other crime scene—methodical, scanning for patterns. But instead of clues and names, only one truth came forth:

Something else is pulling the strings—and has been all along.

CHAPTER 8

Ryan and Finn stepped from the interrogation room, ending the questioning. It was clear that they weren't going to get anything from Chad Harrison. There was something deeply wrong with him—more than Finn realized. This was beyond the scope of a standard FBI team.

Agent Finn gave a quick signal to the officer, who prepared to escort the prisoner back to his cell.

Ryan's watch remained silent as the boy slowly shuffled down the hallway. It hadn't so much as flickered since that brief moment when Harrison met her eyes—when something in him felt wrong. Unnaturally wrong.

Whatever it was, she couldn't explain it. Only that it made her spine tingle and her fingers go numb.

A cold gust drifted down the corridor, stirring Ryan's hair across her shoulders. As the sound of the main doors closing echoed through the station, the heavy scent of rain and wet pavement lingered in the air.

A young woman appeared around the corner from the lobby, hair and clothes soaked and clinging to her slender frame. Her face was reddened by the rain and tears, which left streaks of mascara trailing down her cheeks. Three Greek symbols in white embroidery stood out across her chest.

"Where is he?" she cried out as soon as she saw Ryan.

The girl quickened her pace down the hall, the purse slung over her left shoulder bouncing against her hip. Ryan stepped gently into her path and caught the girl by the arm. Finn moved behind her in case the girl tried to side-step.

"Hey, it's okay," Ryan said calmly. "I'm Special Agent Mills. Can I help you?"

"I need to see Chad." The girl sniffed as tears continued to wet her eyes.

Ryan glanced at Finn but kept her hand lightly on the girl's arm. Her thin limb shivered, and goosebumps rose on her damp skin.

"And who are you?"

"I-I'm Chelsea . . . Chelsea Kenton." Her voice caught on a sob. "I drove all day to get here. I have to help him."

"Okay, Chelsea," Ryan said. "Let's get you some coffee first, okay? Get you dried off. Sound good?"

The girl nodded and sniffed again. Ryan glanced at Finn, who directed them back to the now-empty conference room. Sometime after they'd left to interrogate Harrison, the others had vacated the room.

Ryan pulled out a chair, and Chelsea dropped into it, shoulders slumped and shivering. Water beaded on her tanned skin where a silk bra strap peeked out from the edge of her tank top. Finn reappeared with a hand towel and offered it to Chelsea.

"Thank you," she said softly, dabbing at her dripping hair. He moved around to the other side of the table and shot a glance at Ryan, clearly not expecting this girl to show up, and knew nothing about her. He urged Ryan to talk to her.

"Agent Finn and I have been working with Chad," Ryan said, placing a cup of coffee in front of Chelsea and then taking the seat across from her. The girl looked up, wiping the towel across her shoulders. "You said you wanted to help him. How do you feel you can do that?"

Though her face was dry, the tears still flooded her eyes. "Chad didn't do this. There's no way he could do this. I don't care what the TV is saying about him."

Ryan leaned forward, tilting her head lightly to the left. "Tell me about him."

The girl let out a frustrated sigh and leaned toward her. "He loves his family. I've never seen someone so close to his brothers and sister. And he called his parents every week. We're both at Florida State—he's my boyfriend—and he's on the honor roll for heaven's sake. He's a good person." Chelsea pulled up to the edge of the table and grasped Ryan's hand in a desperate plea. "I know he didn't do this."

Ryan curled her fingers around the girl's grasp. "Chelsea . . . he confessed—"

Chelsea stood up suddenly. "He didn't do it. It was the house!" Her eyes had gone wide.

That was the last thing Ryan had expected to hear. "Please, Chelsea. Sit. What do you mean the house?"

Chelsea sat down, leaning back in the chair again. "Chad hated going there. They spent every spring and summer at that place, and he always hated it."

Finn placed his elbows on the table. "Hated it enough to snap? To do something like this?"

"No!" Her brow furrowed, then she returned her gaze to Ryan. "Not like that. He said it creeped him out to be there. I talked to him the night before this happened—he was fine. We did a video chat and then . . . something weird happened."

Ryan's attention sharpened. "What do you mean, *weird?*"

Chelsea swallowed, her gaze drifting toward the closed door

as if replaying it in her mind. "We were talking like usual, but then he stopped and said the house alarm went off. He left the screen for a moment, and when he came back, he said the exterior motion lights had turned on. All of them. He said they'd been doing that every night." She folded her arms across her torso in a tight embrace. "And there were other things."

"Other things? What did he say, Chelsea?" Ryan leaned closer.

She shook her head, closing her eyes. "He said he sometimes heard voices in the house. Not his family, but someone. When he went to check to see who it was, no one was there. I was afraid that someone had broken into the house and was messing with him. But after last night . . ." Her voice cracked into a sob again. "I knew someone *had* gotten into that house."

Ryan glanced at Finn, who shook his head. If someone else had been there, why would Chad confess to the killings? Why would he wait on the doorstep for the police? It was as if he'd wanted to be caught.

"Okay," Ryan said, standing. "Thank you for the information, Chelsea. We'll look into it. Please wait here, a deputy will be in to take your full statement."

She moved to step out of the room when Chelsea caught her by the wrist. Tear-soaked eyes looked up at her. "I promise you," she whispered, "he didn't do this."

Ryan offered a slight nod, then quietly followed Finn out, closing the conference room doors. He fell into step beside her, hands settling on his hips again.

"There's no way anyone else was involved," he said, keeping his voice low so it wouldn't carry down the hall.

"As soon as my team gets to the scene, I'll have more answers."

"Well, I'll get you in first thing tomorrow. The sheriff will take you to the hotel tonight, and he'll pick you up tomorrow. Keep me updated—and let me know the second you find anything new."

"Likewise."

CHAPTER 9

By the time Ryan reached her motel room, the rain had soaked through every layer of clothing, chilling her to the bone. She'd jogged through the downpour from the car to the outdoor corridor, but now, standing in front of her door, there was no point in rushing—she was already drenched.

The lock clicked with a wave of the key card. The moment Ryan pushed open the door, the adjacent room door opened, and Holbrook peeked around the edge of the frame, the parking lot lights illuminating his smile.

"You're back."

Rain dripped from hair plastered against her forehead. "Yeah, and I'm soaked." A shiver moved over her skin. Too cold to keep up an outdoor conversation, Ryan waved Holbrook toward her room. "Get over here. We need to talk."

Turning on the lights, a trail of water droplets followed her as she walked into the room. Holbrook followed, and the door clicked shut behind him in a quiet click.

"I wasn't sure when you'd be back," he said as Ryan continued across the room. "They wouldn't tell us anything."

The shivering intensified—no time to stop or explain. Without looking back, she plunged into the bathroom, stripping off the damp suit coat as she went. It hit the stone-tiled floor with a wet thud.

"It was interesting, to say the least," she called, fingers fumbling as she tried to unbutton her shirt. Cold fingers trembling with each button, slipping to get them loose.

"I assumed we were going to the crime scene tonight," he said.

Goosebumps tickled over her bare skin, now fully exposed in the air-conditioned bathroom. At least it was well stocked with thick towels. She pulled a soft robe from the silver cubicle shelf and wrapped it around her body, easing the flood of shivers. With a towel in her hand, she emerged from the bathroom.

Holbrook straightened the moment he saw her. "I-I'm sort. I should probably go."

She stopped at the edge of the king-sized bed and leaned forward to dry her hair with the towel. "Why?"

"Well," he said, vaguely motioning in her direction, "you're naked."

She almost laughed. *Must be a British thing.* Or Matt was the most gentlemanly person she'd ever met.

"I'm not naked. This is a robe." She gave a theatrical wave down the length of her torso. "Robes clothe people, thus I'm not naked."

His jaw went slack, and he averted his gaze, as though the lamp on the nightstand was the most interesting thing in the room. Hands disappeared into the pockets of his slacks.

"Matt, sit." Ryan pointed to the small table and chairs at the far end of the room.

He nodded but only flashed her a small glance. Ryan settled into the chair opposite him, tossing the damp towel across the back of her chair.

"I saw him tonight," she started, leaning her elbows onto the surface of the table.

This time, Holbrook met her gaze with fascination. "Harrison?"

She nodded. "Talked to him. Well, *I* talked, he just sat there. It was . . . strange."

"Strange how?"

Her eyes drifted down to the table. Memories of the interrogation came to the surface, as if it had happened mere seconds ago: Chad, sitting across the table, hands in silver wrist cuffs, eyes shadowed by hair. Goosebumps prickled across her arms again, but this time, it wasn't from the cold.

"He was there, sitting right across from me. But it was like . . . he wasn't there. Only a shell." She walked Holbrook through the interrogation in detail, including the appearance of Chad's girlfriend.

When she finished, Holbrook let out a long sigh. "What do you feel about all this?"

"I mean, he confessed—"

"No," Matt interrupted gently. "That's not what I mean. What do you *feel?*"

She knew what he'd meant. Ever since discovering her ability, it had been something unspoken between them until they both needed it.

This was one of those moments.

Sitting across from Chad Harrison had felt unusual at the time, but was that because of what she knew he'd done less than twenty-four hours earlier? If she'd been at the crime scene, maybe her reaction would have been clearer. She shook her head. *It wasn't about his actions then.* It was his absence, now. His dead-eyed stare. The sudden, unnatural shift in his body.

And then there was her wrist monitor.

She pulled back the sleeve of her robe, revealing the watch, still intact despite the torrential storm outside.

"I activated this before I went in," she said, tapping the black screen. "It was all crickets until I suggested that he didn't want to kill his family. Then it lit up and wouldn't stop."

Creases formed at the corners of Holbrook's eyes. "Interesting."

"And it was the only time he reacted to anything I said."

He nodded, looking at his hands that now rested on the table.

"What does that mean?" she asked.

"I'm not sure, but we should proceed with caution."

Ryan brushed the curtain of long, damp hair from her shoulder and let it fall back. "They're letting us into the crime scene in the morning. The sheriff will be here at eight. We need to get some sleep until then."

"Yes," he said and stood. "Call me if you need anything in the meantime. You know where I am." He ticked his head to the wall across the room and smiled.

"I do."

He was halfway to the door when Ryan spoke again.

"There's one more thing," she said. "The girlfriend mentioned something interesting—that Chad hated the house. Said it creeped him out. She thought someone might have been trying to scare them."

Holbrook nodded. "Okay, I'll look into it. Maybe there's something in the property records or local history that I can research. Good work." He flashed her another smile. "Sleep well."

"Thanks. You too."

But she hadn't slept well for months. Tonight wouldn't be any different. There were plenty of lights to leave on all night, and sleeping pills weren't an option. Not tonight. She needed to be sharp tomorrow. For Emma's sake.

She watched Holbrook open the door, feeling a faint tug in her chest as he stepped away.

"Hey, Matt," she said, faster than she had expected. He turned back, eyebrows raised. But her mouth had gone dry, and whatever thought she'd meant to say evaporated. So, she said the first thing she could think of. "Have a good night."

His expression softened. He gave a slight nod before slipping out of the room. The door clicked closed, and Ryan was alone for the first time in so many hours. She slid between the slick white bed linens, warmth returning to her body. The shivers had stopped, but a quaking continued deep within her gut, increasing in intensity every time she closed her eyes and saw Chad Harrison's quiet form across the table. Staring blankly from behind a curtain of dark hair.

He was there, but he wasn't.

Yesterday, upon the stair, I met a man who wasn't there.

No. Not again. Ever since Summer's whirlwind session on how to get the poem out of her brain, they kept popping back in with a vengeance. Word for word, like the written message from Lexi's killer. The man who wasn't there. But he was *always*, always in her thoughts, night after night.

She crawled across the bed to the nightstand, grabbed the remote control, and snapped on the television. She frantically clicked through the stations to find anything that would take away the voice that recited that damned poem over and over in her brain. Home renovation shows and political pundits arguing back and forth. She clicked through the channels until the voice quieted enough to ease the shaking in her hands.

Tears welled at the edge of her eyes, but she blinked them away. *There's nothing wrong. Only memories. Stupid, damned horrible memories.* They would be gone by morning.

She had to make it until then.

CHAPTER 10

Ryan was out of bed and staring at her tangle of blonde hair in the bathroom mirror when the knock came at the door. Maybe it was the hour or two of restless sleep she got last night, but the searing white overhead lights burned into her eyes.

She glanced toward the door, knowing exactly who stood on the other side.

Swallowing back the dryness in her throat, she pulled it open. Bright spears of morning sunlight, bursting through breaks in the dark clouds, cut into her vision. Shielding her eyes from the onslaught, she saw a blurred form standing before her, steam rising from a cup of fragrant coffee.

"Morning, Sheriff," she croaked.

"Special Agent Mills." Watson stretched out a hand holding the coffee.

"Thank you," she said, accepting the drink with both hands. The rich scent filled her nose, and it met her lips with a welcome burn.

"Oh my goodness, this is so awesome." She smiled, then gave an appreciative nod. "Give me five more minutes and I'll be right out."

The door slipped from her hand and shut with a thud much louder than intended.

She winced. The sheriff, waiting on the pavement outside,

would have to understand. She wasn't at her best after last night, but with enough coffee and a quick shower, she'd be semi-functional.

Five minutes had turned into seven, but Ryan finally stepped out with the remainder of the beverage and her hair tied into a messy bun. The cool morning air hung heavy with the scent of last night's rain. Her dark blue parka, draped across her arm, would come in handy.

Two vehicles waited in the parking lot: a plain white van and the sheriff's SUV. The crew had already loaded most of the equipment into the van.

"Alright," Watson said, zipping up the front of his dark brown jacket embroidered with his name and SHERIFF emblazoned across the back. "Special Agent Mills, if you wouldn't mind riding with me, I can get you up to date."

He glanced back at Holbrook. "You can follow us."

The others nodded, and Watson climbed into the SUV with Mills. He fired up the engine, and the vehicle rolled out of the parking lot and onto the road, passing under rows of overhanging tree branches heavy with moisture. Large puddles shimmered along the edge of the street—some stretching across the black pavement, their rippling surfaces reflecting gray clouds that warned of more rain to come.

For now, the golden sunlight that pierced through the canopy cut across the wet ground like pale fingers reaching for something already gone.

Sheriff Watson drove along the highway as the town of Currant Falls thinned to a few houses and green fields, which soon gave way to dense trees. The SUV turned onto a side road that plunged them into the dark forest.

"What do you know about the Harrison mansion?" Watson asked, breaking the quiet after Mills finished the last of her coffee.

She cleared her throat. "Not much, truthfully. Only what I've found online. The department's brief was mostly focused on the individual crime scenes."

"Well," he started, "the reason the search is so difficult is because of the size of the estate. Luckily, you have me." He flashed her a smile beneath his scruffy, unshaven face.

Ryan raised an eyebrow. "You know about the place?"

"I used to work there in the summers when I was younger."

"What, like as a groundskeeper or something?"

"Nope. Tour guide. The estate is listed on the historic registrar, and the Harrisons were proud of that. They traveled a lot, so they'd open the place for limited tours during the summer."

Her stomach tightened. That meant hundreds, if not thousands, of people had seen the mansion's interior and were familiar with its layout. This investigation suddenly got a lot harder.

"It's one of those places from the old days of grand design, originally built in 1889," he continued. "There are over 250 rooms, and that's only in the main house."

"And how much of that was open to the public?" she asked.

"Twenty of the main rooms. The tour of the mansion ran about an hour to an hour and a half. Then some of the grounds. Rarely any of the third or fourth floor rooms except for VIP tours."

The coffee in her stomach turned bitter. "There's more than just a house?"

"There's the mansion, a stable, a greenhouse, a staff house, and a lot of other old buildings. Most aren't used anymore, but they're still part of the historic estate, which sits on over 63,000 acres, most of which is forest."

Sheriff Watson paused, then added. "Oh, and there's the lake."

"This keeps getting better," she muttered. Every time

Watson said anything, her imagination swarmed with images of sprawling land and endless architecture that expanded and pulled away like a satellite image.

"Where are they with the search?"

"The house has been searched from top to bottom, thanks to the FBI. I didn't have enough manpower to search that much area. The outbuildings have all been checked. Right now, dog teams are combing the woods, but that could take days. The lake hasn't been dredged yet. They held off, waiting to see what your team finds."

A bitter burn rose in her throat. Somewhere out there—alive or dead—Emma Harrison was lost in that vast expanse of a billionaire's estate. And after last night's cold downpour, any trace of her would be harder to find.

Watson maneuvered the SUV along the winding road. Sunlight that had punctuated the post-monsoon morning was now hidden behind a barrier of overhanging trees, leaving the road in a twilight of damp earth and black puddles.

The tree line broke, and sunlight returned, illuminating the start of a massive brick wall that stretched out alongside the road as far as she could see. It blocked their view of anything beyond, teasing them until they reached a towering iron gate. Gleaming in the center of the two closed doors sat a massive silver sculpture of the sun.

Mills hadn't detected any police presence until now. A dozen or more official vehicles were parked along the side of the road just outside the wall, and more were visible along the driveway that plunged deeper into the property.

An agent in a navy-blue jacket came into view. The moment he laid eyes on the sheriff's SUV, he nodded, and the gate opened with a low, electric hum. Watson eased forward and then rolled down the window as the agent stepped up to the car.

"Agent Finn is waiting for you at the main house, sir." The agent flashed a glance at Ryan. "They're wrapping up and will be evacuating soon. Everything's ready for your team."

"Thank you, Agent." Ryan nodded.

Cold air rushed into the SUV before Watson could seal the window. More trees lined the road, their trunks shadowing the oily, black pavement, still wet with last night's storm. Groomed lawns stretched beyond the tree line, dotted occasionally with brick pedestals topped by lamps, now silent in the pale morning.

The car rolled forward, and with every passing tree, Ryan's chest grew tighter. Somewhere beyond this immaculate landscape sat the Harrison mansion—its unseen arms reaching out through the thick forests, across the lake, and bleeding into the cold morning air.

The road finally pierced through the row of trees, and she got her first glimpse of the mansion. Nothing could have prepared Ryan for the sheer scale of it. Emotionless photos hadn't come close to capturing the impact of viewing the structure in person.

It stood like a monolith at the end of a road that curved around a large, manicured, green lawn. Turrets rose into the sky like sentinels atop the four stories of windows. The pale gray stone walls carried climbing arms of ivy that reached the highest levels, including the dark edges of the roof.

And at its center, a grand entryway jutted out toward the drive with stone pillars supporting an awning that sheltered a set of double doors.

Ryan stepped from the vehicle, her eyes never leaving the building. It loomed above her, stately and beautiful, but each window gazed at her with dark and empty eyes.

Eyes as dark as Chad Harrison's were in the police interrogation room.

No amount of morning light could illuminate those windows. Nor could it take the chill from her bones as she scanned the mansion's massive structure. The building pulled her into its girth and held her like a statue, frozen and timeless.

"I'll take you inside, Special Agent Mills," Watson said, waiting beneath the awning.

Her feet wouldn't move. The moment she entered, she knew it would consume her—like an open door to a walk-in freezer. As soon as you step inside, it smothers you with cold. But Watson motioned her to follow up the short flight of stairs to the entrance.

And Emma waited for her out here, somewhere.

Ryan tentatively followed, one step at a time, until Watson gave the doors a shove. A rush of warm air brushed past her from inside the atrium, thick with the scent of history and secrets.

The sheriff continued to talk, more details about the house and the interior, but she no longer heard him. Crossing the threshold was like being swallowed. The entry gave way to dark mahogany-paneled walls and a towering marble statue of a Greek goddess, standing like a ghostly tongue in the rich mouth of the mansion.

But the grandeur was quickly shattered. A single bloody footprint, congealed and dark, stained the marble tile, next to a vibrant crime scene marker.

Stepping carefully around the evidence, Ryan followed Watson through the atrium and into the body of the house. The room opened into a vast central hall with corridors stretching to the left and right. A grand staircase rising from the center of the room spiraled upward through all four floors.

At the top, a domed skylight of intricate glass panels filtered sunlight into the space. At night, the chandelier suspended from the dome would likely illuminate the space with an ethereal gold light through a shower of crystals that dangled from each bulb.

The same dark mahogany that greeted her in the atrium stretched along the walls, becoming part of the polished handrails of the staircase.

This was the most opulent place she'd ever seen that was called a *home*. And now it was a crime scene. Scene tags dotted the staircase, most likely indicating more bloody footprints.

The air was much warmer than the cool of the morning outside, yet a chill crawled along her forearms. Thoughts swam through her brain. She tried to focus on Watson's voice, but she couldn't connect fast enough before the images flooded her mind, and the scene transformed.

The room flashed into darkness. It was night. The lights were out, and only the occasional burst of lightning illuminated the scene through the dome's glass panels—the dome above *him*.

The figure descended the stairs, shotgun in his right hand, the barrel tapping lightly against his leg with each step. The front of his long pajama pants dripped with blood. More was splattered across his shirt. Blank, lifeless eyes quickly locked onto Ryan as he reached the landing.

The same eyes she'd seen across the interrogation table. Empty. Wrong.

"Special Agent Mills?" Watson's voice rang out, echoing through the cavernous room.

The image of Chad shattered. Light returned. And her breath caught in her throat when she finally saw the sheriff.

"You alright?" he asked, brow creased.

She gave a tight nod. "Fine. Just taking it all in. And . . . call me Ryan."

"Great." He followed her gaze up to the stairs. "I'll take you to where it all happened."

He started up the stairs, stepping carefully around the evidence markers. Ryan tried to follow, but her feet froze. The air chilled again, and goosebumps rose under her thin shirt. She knew the Harrisons' son wasn't there, nor was he coming back. But the echo of what had happened infected everything in this place.

As she placed a boot on the first step, something shifted behind her.

It was the slightest sound. A whisper of movement—like a curtain rustling in a breeze, or a plant twitching under an air vent. She stopped.

'Don't go,' a child's voice whispered.

Emma! Ryan's heart lurched.

Ryan turned slowly, deliberately. The sound had been soft, so soft that Cole Watson, now climbing to the second floor, hadn't noticed. But she had.

She scanned the landing. Empty. Yet the whisper prickled the hairs on her neck. Her gaze swept the right corridor. Nothing. When she glanced to the left, a small figure darted down the hall and out of view, leaving only a small wet footprint behind.

Ryan jumped from the stairs and rushed to the hallway entrance.

"Emma? Wait. Please," she whispered.

The hallway stretched deep into the heart of the mansion, bathed in filtered light from the dozens of tall windows. The same hardwood floors gleamed beneath her boots, and dark mahogany panels framed the walls. On one side stood marble statues and soft upholstered chairs with side tables. On the other, doors to various rooms.

But no small figure. No child. No Emma Harrison.

"Ryan?" Watson's voice called to her again.

Her heart pounded. That wasn't one of her visions, at least she didn't think it was. Had this place gotten her so anxious that she only imagined the child?

"You coming?" She stepped back and glanced up the spiral staircase where Watson leaned over the banister.

"Yes." Ryan scanned the corridor one last time, listening for anything else that might call out to her. Yet, as she started to climb the stairs, a whisper echoed in her mind—

Don't go.

CHAPTER 11

Ryan stepped onto the third-floor landing, her fingers trailing along the smooth curve of the polished, wooden banister. She let go before it curved around into an overlook that offered a dizzying view straight down to the atrium below.

But she didn't look.

She kept moving, the chill of the child's unearthly voice still brushing at the back of her neck, like a phantom hand. It tugged at her in a way she couldn't describe.

Not a vision. Not a memory. This was different. Like a thread deep within her was being gently but insistently tugged.

Don't go.

The whisper lingered—soft, persistent—like it had taken root beneath her thoughts.

Ryan stepped past Cole in silence, scanning the corridors that stretched into the east and west wings of the mansion. She could sense . . . *something.* What she didn't know, but she knew its fading presence lay within the shadows. Just out of reach.

Long, oriental-style rugs ran the length of the hallway's dark, hardwood floors. Soft morning light shone through the southern-facing windows, but seemed muted. Maybe it was the effect of the lower ceiling . . . or the way the carpet swallowed the sound. And similar to the lower levels, closed doors lined the north wall.

As she fixated on the west hallway, Cole's muffled footsteps behind her drifted through the corridor and down the staircase.

"Hey, Dr. Holbrook," the sheriff called, catching Ryan's attention. She glanced over her shoulder to see him leaning over the banister. "There's an elevator to the third floor around the corner to your right. Bring the equipment up that way."

Watson turned back to her, stuffing his hands into the pockets of his jeans. "Okay, so this was the main living floor. The family's private space. And," he said, ticking his chin toward the hallway behind her, "that is where it all happened."

"From outside, I counted four floors," Ryan said.

Cole nodded. "The attic, above us. Staircases at the end of both the east and west wings. The doors were locked but the entire space was checked out. The entire house was searched from top to bottom. No sign of the girl."

Trauma clung to the walls like static, coursing along the walls and floorboards, imprinting into the floorboards, pulsing in the air. A lasting imprint of death. And lurking around the east hall corner, it waited.

Ryan shook her head. *Enough.*

Drawing in a slow breath, she closed her eyes. She pictured a wall, just as Summer had instructed—light like glass, solid like stone. It rose up between her and the energy of this place.

I am in control. No more distractions. No more invisible threads.

"Enough," she whispered.

"Agent Mills?"

Ryan opened her eyes to find Sheriff Watson watching her, one brow raised. She scanned the corridor again. Just a hallway. Hardwood. Wallpaper. Light. No more tugging.

Well, that was easy.

"All good," she said with a smug nod.

The elevator doors hissed open, and Holbrook stepped into the west corridor, his usual grin tinged with apprehension. And with good reason. Lazarus had never been used in this capacity before. Despite their hopes of a good outcome, no one could guarantee they'd find anything useful.

Usually, they entered the crime scene, and Lazarus reconstructed the past: the weapon, the manner of death. Sometimes, the perpetrator. Simple cold, clinical facts. In this case, they already knew what had happened to the Harrisons.

To all but one.

"Follow me. I'll show you the first location," Cole offered.

Ryan stopped him. "Sheriff, my team will take it from here, if you don't mind."

His jaw tightened, but he gave a nod. "Okay. I'll . . . wait here in case you need anything." He leaned back against the banister.

Holbrook glanced over his shoulder at Coti and Dave. "Go ahead and bring up the rest of the equipment, and we'll set up outside the first scene."

Then he turned to Ryan, his familiar grin playing over his lips. "Lead the way."

She didn't need Watson to show her where the crime had occurred. The buzzing in her chest and tremble of her fingers guided the path.

As she stepped into the east wing corridor, the morning light dimmed around her, giving way to night. White curtains faded to shadow, and sunlight was replaced by bursts of lightning. The storm. The murder night. Barely thirty-six hours ago.

Another flash lit the hall, illuminating a set of open double doors. A memory she'd never lived played through her mind like a reel-to-reel film.

She envisioned both realities simultaneously—the room as it was, and as it had been.

The curtains now hung partially open, letting in enough pale sunlight to chase away the stillness that rested here. Ryan smelled the blood before she saw it, a heavy, cloying odor that hit her the moment she crossed the threshold. A king-sized bed rested at one end of the room, its linens strewn in a heap at the foot of the bed. On the opposite wall, a seventy-two-inch television perched above the bureau. The blood hadn't reached that far. It had pooled in two heavy puddles of crimson upon the white sheets and pillows.

Flash.

Ryan watched the room plunge into darkness. Two people lay in the bed—a man and a woman, both in deep sleep. Then the door opened. Slow. Deliberate.

Chad stood in the doorway, his form a shadow, face unreadable. His t-shirt and long pajama pants clean, spotless. A shotgun hung along his right leg, the barrel pointing to the floor. Rumbling thunder shook the house, but Chad didn't move. Another burst of lightning illuminated his face—blank and empty.

Then it was gone. The storm vanished, and the room again filled with morning light. Holbrook stood in the doorway, watching her with curiosity.

"What do you see, Ryan?" his voice was low enough so that the others wouldn't hear.

"The Harrisons sleeping. A major storm is happening outside. And Chad opens the door. This is the first place he stopped."

The memory gripped her again. Chad stood inside the room, staring at his parents. The weight of the shotgun pulled his right arm down enough that his shoulders rested offset. What was he waiting for? Ryan watched him for several moments, then realized something deeply unnerving about his gaze.

He never blinked.

A lightning flash momentarily filled the room in bright, electric light. Yet, an unearthly shimmer lingered in his eyes long after the room had returned to shadow.

Then he moved. His trance broken by the rolling thunder, Chad lifted the shotgun and cocked it with a sharp click. His father stirred but didn't fully wake. The boy strode forward, the gun now in both hands, and approached the edge of the bed. The gun came up, butt of the stock pressed firmly against his right shoulder, and he aimed the barrel at his father's head.

The shot exploded with such violence that Ryan gasped. She turned toward Holbrook as the acrid odor of gunpowder and blood filled her nostrils. "He killed his father first."

Chad's mother jerked upright—in time to see the double-barreled gun turn toward her. Her hands flew up to cover her face, and the weapon fired again. Light bloomed at the end of the gun, and the woman slumped on the bed, her face now a cavern of darkness.

Blood splattered across her son's clothes like droplets of thick, dark oil—the first stains of what the night had planned.

Ryan gagged, covering her mouth. She'd investigated dozens of murders—brutal, chaotic, senseless. But this . . . this was different. Even with Stephen Jeffries' murder, the killers had *felt* something. But Chad? He just stood there, motionless, clutching his weapon, as if an empty shell. No panic. No fear. No satisfaction. No reaction at all.

Nothing except the faint silver reflection deep within his eyes.

Ryan watched for what felt like an eternity before the boy turned and marched out the door, the sound of the gun cocking echoing down the hallway with each retreating footstep.

Darkness faded to morning light again.

"Are you alright?" Holbrook asked.

Ryan focused on Matt's face. The curve of his jawline. His hair. Anything to ground her to the present. "I-I don't know. This was . . . intense."

"What happened?"

A shudder ran down her spine. "His mother. She woke up before it happened. She *saw* him."

He hung his head and studied his shoes, something he did when composing his thoughts. "I'm sorry you had to see that."

"But I *didn't* see Emma." Ryan quickly glanced around the room. There was no sign that the youngest Harrison had been there. At least that gave her hope. "If Chad had killed his sister in the same manner as he did the rest of his family, they would've found evidence on his clothes. But they didn't. And when he walked into his parents' bedroom, his clothes were spotless."

She turned to Holbrook. "Start setting up in here and get Lazarus running. We'll go room to room if we have to. She has to be somewhere."

When Holbrook left, her watch began to vibrate. She frowned and reluctantly glanced toward the bed, but no visions followed. She tapped the black watch face, wondering if Holbrook's new tech had glitched.

"Why are you here?" came a voice from the doorway—refined, distinctively British with a slightly worn edge.

The tension in Ryan's shoulders eased, replaced with

irritation. This wasn't the time for one of Matt's cryptic discussions. "You know why *I'm* here, Doc." She turned to face him, spine straightening. "The question is why you aren't setting up the equipment and—"

The threshold stood empty, with only wisps of morning light falling into the barren corridor outside the bedroom. The buzzing of the watch stopped. Now, she was even more annoyed with the games. It was too early, and she wasn't in the mood to do this with Holbrook today.

She hurried to the door, gripping the frame as she swung into the hall in time to see a man, not Holbrook, walking away. The stranger's steps were steady, unhurried, and his black, well-fitted suit hung from narrow shoulders beneath pepper-gray hair. The right arm was bent at the elbow and was draped with a white linen cloth.

"Hey! Wait a Minute!" Ryan called.

No response. The man simply kept walking down the hallway.

"Stop," she called out again. "How did you get in here?"

"You're not supposed to be here. The house is closed to visitors," he repeated, continuing to pace away. His casual glance at each door he passed proved that either he never heard her.

"Did you say something?" Holbrook called from another room farther down the corridor.

Ryan turned to see Matt peering around the edge of a door to a different room. "Yeah," she pointed back down the hall to the man in the suit. "I think he broke into the house."

"Who?" Holbrook's dark eyebrows furrowed, and his left eye squinted slightly.

"That guy." She turned to point, but the man in the suit was gone. "Wait a second," she muttered. Is he hiding in one of the other rooms? She rushed down the hall. The row of doors on the right opened with ease, revealing dark, curtained rooms devoid of life.

"No," she muttered again. The guy couldn't have made it to the end of the hallway and to the landing in the few seconds she had her back turned.

Holbrook appeared at her side. "Whom did you see?" His voice had fallen to that private whisper he used when referring to her abilities.

"He was here. He talked to me." She hadn't imagined it. "There was a man in a suit, as real as you or I. He looked like a butler and seemed upset that I was in that room."

"There's nobody else here but us," Holbrook said quietly. "The FBI closed the grounds to everyone except our team. Did you see . . . something else?"

Shafts of dusty light slanted through the windows, casting alternating patches of light and dark. The man—whatever he was—had vanished into those shadowy spaces, lost in some part of the house neither she nor Holbrook could access.

Ryan glanced at the now-silent watch. It buzzed the very moment the man spoke. Why? She wasn't sure who the man was or where he had gone. One thing was sure: someone else was in the house, and that someone wanted them out.

CHAPTER 12

Ryan logged into the main Lazarus program on one of the laptops set up across the table in the master bedroom. After closing all the curtains to darken the room, Coti stepped around the tripod holding the mini-Lazarus device in the center of the room to secure the last of the cords.

From the corner of her eye, Ryan noticed Coti and Dave attempting not to look at the bloodstained sheets on the bed—but they were difficult to avoid. The scene itself was the reason they were here.

Dave's fingers played across his keyboard before punching *Enter* with a sharp tap. "Okay, we're in and ready to roll. Cameras ready?"

Ryan and Coti nodded. The screen displayed four camera angles, each carefully positioned to capture anything Lazarus might reveal.

"Okay, Doc." Dave glanced at Holbrook, who stood against the wall with his arms folded across his chest.

"And where's our trusty Sheriff Watson?" Holbrook said.

"Sent him downstairs to wait," Coti spoke, a slight smile tugging at the corner of her mouth. "Top secret. Need-to-know."

Holbrook took in a steady breath, then pushed off the wall. "Then let's begin."

Coti distributed the clear-lens spectacles. Ryan slid hers into place, not that she needed them. The others required the glasses to interpret what Lazarus revealed, but whenever the device fired up, it had a way of reaching her directly. The moment it powered on, the hidden world awakened—showing things only she could see.

"Here we go." Dave's finger hovered above the *Enter* key again. "Three . . . two . . . one." With a sharp flick of his wrist, the key clicked, and Lazarus came to life.

Blue light exploded across the room in a sweeping grid of laser light that enveloped the entire room. Ryan stood still, knowing that Lazarus wouldn't show her anything she didn't already know. That seemed to happen a lot these days. But maybe it would pick up on something she couldn't see. That was the hope. That it could see Emma, alive or dead.

The grid settled to the ground, and the light blinked like an old television trying to catch a stray signal. It coalesced into a fuzzy, static blue light that danced into the shadows, flickering across the walls and furniture until it finally stopped at the bed.

Two ghostly figures appeared: Mr. Harrison and his wife.

Lazarus picked up on every residual trace of energy imprinted in the space—and the strongest impressions always came from the dead. Their presence was vivid, like a pained, final memory that was sealed into the room's bones.

Ryan saw the scene play out, just as she'd witnessed earlier when the room's energy had surrounded her. As the others watched, the blue glare of the grid light reflecting on their glasses, she turned and glanced toward the bedroom door.

Empty.

She half-expected, half-hoped to see the strange man again, silently watching, telling them that they didn't belong. But the doorway remained barren. She lingered a moment longer before turning back to the hologram in the room.

Lazarus showed everything. The horror. The silence. The truth.

But it couldn't express the way Chad's eyes gazed at his sleeping parents. How cold and distant he was when he stood there and shot them. Every second of the playback was recorded to the computer. But it didn't show Emma. The little girl hadn't entered the room when her parents were murdered.

At least that was a small bit of comfort.

Ryan helped pack up the equipment, then made her way down the hall to a room she hadn't visited yet. She wasn't looking forward to what was next. The murders of Chad's two younger brothers, ages nine and thirteen. Visions she didn't want etched into her mind. But they had to use Lazarus here, too. They had to see it play out in case there was any sign of Emma.

And like in the master bedroom, Lazarus did its job. Sometimes too well. Ryan turned away when Chad raised the shotgun toward the nine-year-old. She didn't need to see the rest. She'd felt it the moment she entered the room, and that was enough.

The recording continued. Every moment captured, but still no sign of the youngest Harrison child.

They finished setting up in the third room, the bedroom of the thirteen-year-old son. Soccer trophies lined a shelf above the bed. Posters of his favorite soccer players plastered the walls.

"Manchester United," Holbrook muttered with his hands stuffed into his pockets.

"What is that?" Ryan asked, stepping next to him.

He pointed to the first poster, a frozen action shot of a soccer player mid-strike, long blonde hair flying behind him as he readied his foot to move the ball. "Manchester United. My favorite team, too."

A lump rose in Ryan's throat. The comment was unexpectedly tender, revealing a small flicker of the boy's life before everything was shattered.

Then she swallowed back the bile, because beneath that poster, a few feet from where she and Matt stood, she could smell the blood. It had splattered in a violent arc across the wall, and she knew that if anyone looked closely, they'd see more than just blood. The entire, horrifying truth of what had been lost.

The room darkened and, once again, Ryan watched the scene unfold. The boy had heard the last three gunshots that night. Nicholas, but everyone called him Nick. The sharp rapports startled him awake, but he had thought they were firecrackers. Nothing to worry about when the door opened, it was only Chad. Probably checking on him to make sure he was okay. The sounds must have woken him up, too.

Nick sat up in bed. He didn't really see the shotgun rise in Chad's hand. There was something in his brother's hands, but he didn't know what it was. The last thing he saw was the bright flare from the gun barrel.

Ryan flinched, feeling it the way he had. Quick pain, then nothing. Blackness.

The blood spatter was different here. Nick had been sitting upright. Awake when it had happened.

Again, Ryan turned away when Lazarus played it back. She didn't need to rewatch the horror. Only Holbrook noticed. He always did. She tried not to show the others. When she felt it was over, she glanced back during the final moment, long enough to see Chad lower the smoking gun and walk away through the open door.

And still no sign of Emma.

The child hadn't witnessed any of the murders, but was it because she was actually the first?

The fourth Lazarus set up was in the youngest child's room. A menagerie of stuffed animals filled the space—puppies, kittens, penguins, elephants, lobsters, and unicorns. Nearly every surface held some treasured creature. Emma Harrison loved animals. That much was clear.

Pink, frilly linens covered the bed and had been pulled back. The faint impression in the rumpled sheets suggested a small body had once lain there in quiet slumber.

"No blood," Ryan said, her voice low as the others set up the computers at the edge of the room. Her eyes moved slowly around the space. No residual energy. No lingering shadows. Only the soft, undisturbed signs that a five-year-old girl had been sleeping here . . . and then she wasn't.

Holbrook stepped up beside her. "You getting anything?" he whispered.

Ryan shook her head. "Nothing."

And Lazarus agreed. Its scans flickered with their usual static, but nothing materialized—no trace of a death imprint.

"She's not here," Dave said, leaning forward, his elbows on the table. "So, where did she go?"

"I doubt she could have outrun him," Coti said.

Ryan stared at the empty bed. "Maybe she didn't have to."

Holbrook tilted his head. "What are you thinking?"

"Let's say, she heard the shots. There were at least four of them that could have woken her up at any time." Ryan paced toward the bed. "We know that the last victim, Nick, was awake. Maybe she woke up, too."

"She hears the shots and gets out of bed," Ryan said, walking toward the exit, "and looks down the hallway."

The hall stretched almost endlessly in both directions from the child's bedroom door, giving a clear view of anyone in the corridor.

Ryan points down the passageway. "She hears another one. Maybe she sees Chad go into a room. She's smart enough to know something isn't right, so she runs."

"She runs." Holbrook says, following her gaze. "Hides. Somewhere in the house or on the grounds."

Ryan nodded. "I hope so."

"But, the FBI already searched the entire house from top to bottom," Dave said.

"Most of the grounds, too," Coti added.

Ryan turned back to them. "Growing up on my grandparent's ranch, I had a lot of hiding places that nobody else knew about, not even my sister. I could've hidden for hours and nobody would've known."

Holbrook's jaw tightened. "We need Sheriff Watson to give a tour of the grounds. Now."

The familiar smell of horse manure hit them long before they reached the stable doors. Watson heaved one door open along a single metal track, its groan echoing as it slid back to reveal a long central walk that traversed the length of the structure. Ryan stepped inside. She was used to barns, but nothing this size. The stables back home had only three stalls, and this place held twenty or more.

Yet, it was quiet.

"Where are all the animals?"

"FBI took them out yesterday morning," Watson replied. "As soon as they brought in the search dogs, everyone got agitated—horses, hounds, even the handlers."

Ryan glanced up at the second-floor outcrops at both ends of the building. "And the dogs searched through everything, including the hay lofts?"

"They tried," he sighed. "Even after the horses were removed, the dogs were useless. Like they didn't want to be in here." He met her gaze. "I walked the FBI through the whole place. I know this building better than most people. Even the Harrisons." He glanced at Ryan, who responded with a crooked eyebrow. "Seriously. Everything. Tack rooms, storage, crawl spaces—you name it. If there is a place to hide in here, I'd know about it."

Ryan turned back to face the wise expanse of the estate. Through the open doors, the morning light has shifted to a midday haze, and they had gotten nowhere. She sighed. The best she could report to Agent Finn and Director Price was that they knew what *hadn't* happened.

Coti stood with Holbrook a few feet outside the stable doors when Ryan and the sheriff emerged.

Squinting into the sun, she scanned the few buildings beyond the stables. "We'll keep going. Coti. Doc. Go ahead and set up here, do a recording, see what we get," Ryan instructed.

Holbrook took a step forward, his arms crossed over his chest. The curve of his brow left a dark shadow over his eyes. "Do you expect we'll get something here?"

A faint sigh fell from her lips, something she hadn't even intended to do. "I'd be surprised if you did."

She turned to follow Watson when it happened.

Drip.

Just once.

A wet pat against the concrete floor. Like water falling from a great height.

She paused, then rushed back into the stable, scanning the rafters and hayloft. Probably a leak. The roof was old, after all.

Still, the hair on her arms lifted in silent warning.

She checked her watch. Nothing.

"Agent Mills?" Watson called. "Shall we continue?"

She turned to leave.

Drip.

Again. Faint, deliberate.

She froze.

"Is something wrong, Agent Mills?"

She waved in response.

"What is it?" Holbrook asked, Coti pausing in the Lazarus setup.

"I'm not sure," she said, her eyes sweeping the shadows once more. "But do a thorough sweep. Every dark corner."

Holbrook and Coti offered a quick nod, their expressions indecipherable.

As Ryan hurried to catch up with Sheriff Watson, a sound remained behind.

Drip.

They walked along the paved road that curved around the stables and to a collection of smaller structures tucked into the trees. One was clearly a greenhouse, a single rectangular room with glass walls and an A-frame roof. Nothing but light and leaves inside.

"That was the original servant's house," Watson said, pointing to a building beyond the greenhouse. "It's mostly used for storage now."

What passed for a place to shelter the mansion's help looked like a comfortable home for at least two families, if not more.

The three-story, brick colonial rose from a grove of maple trees. White lacy curtains softened the dark windows, and a wide porch encircling the structure beckoned them toward the front door.

The fading warmth of the day cooled Ryan's skin as they neared the porch steps. Her eyes drifted upward to the second story, where every window seemed to stare with indifference as they reflected warped images of the estate.

But her gaze stopped at the third-floor window just above the porch, where a face with a pair of haunting eyes stared back. A woman, her gaunt skin appearing white through the glass, held back the lace curtain with a thin hand.

The watch on Ryan's wrist buzzed, but she didn't look away. The woman's hair, the same shade of blonde as Ryan's, was pulled tight under a white linen cap that tied beneath her chin. The attire appeared similar to that of Amish women or from the eighteenth century. Her dark, long-sleeved dress blurred into the shadows of the room, making it seem as if she was floating in a dark void.

"Everything okay?" Watson asked.

She blinked but didn't lower her eyes. Not this time.

"Yeah," she breathed, though it felt more like she was answering the woman's silent question. "I'm good."

"You see something up there?" He glanced at the third-floor windows.

"Not sure." Of course she was sure, and the watch's constant buzzing confirmed that Holbrook knew what he was doing when he built it.

Watson moved closer, lowering his voice in a reverence. "They say this place is haunted. Not only this house, but the entire estate."

Ryan kept her eyes fixed on the woman.

"I used to be one of the guides for the October tours—not

only during the summer," Watson continued. "The historical society charged extra for their haunted night tours, where we'd share creepy stories passed down over the years under the cover of darkness. Nothing really happened during the tours, but . . ." He paused, staring back at the servant's house. "Sometimes, after hours, when we had to close everything up by ourselves, that's when weird stuff started to happen."

He gestured toward the house. "There was one story I remember of a girl that killed herself after finding out she was pregnant. That happened long before all of this was the estate it is now. Even before the mansion was built. This place was built in 1737. And then the rest grew up around it."

The woman in the window moved for the first time since Ryan had seen her. She shifted her gaze toward the sheriff before stepping away from the window and letting the curtain fall.

The watch's buzzing stopped, but Ryan kept her focus glued on the window for several moments. But the woman didn't return.

Beside her, the sheriff cleared his throat. "Drafty old place. Probably a loose window up there."

Ryan turned toward the sheriff. "She looked at you."

His jaw tightened, then his voice dropped. "I've learned it's best *not* to acknowledge them. Once you do . . ." He shook his head.

She understood. More than he realized.

"So, shall we go inside?" He gestured toward the front door.

She nodded. "I imagine it has already been searched?"

"Thoroughly. By me and several from the FBI. All three floors. The attic. The cellar. Every cupboard and crawl space. If Emma was in there, we'd have found her."

"I'll still have my team come over when they're done with the stables," she said. "Maybe we'll find something."

Watson squinted, the wrinkles around his nose deepening, making him appear much older than he was. "I've got to ask— what exactly are you guys are doing? What is all that stuff that you brought?"

"I told you, it's classified."

Watson gave a lop-sided grin. "Ah, come on. Professional courtesy. Are you guys some high-tech crime scene analysts or something?"

"Something like that."

"That's all I'm gonna get, huh?" His grin widened, then he turned. "Alright, back to the tour."

Cole walked toward a cluster of buildings behind the servant's house. "Those are the gardener's sheds, and that is the old well house."

The structures sat nestled in the trees that overlooked the lake. The gardener's buildings, three boxy, weathered structures, no more than eight feet squared, appeared recently renovated. Yet, the well house stood apart, choked with overgrown ivy and the old wooden doors gray with centuries of abuse.

"And yes, *all* were searched."

"Including the interior of the well house?" The door was sealed by a heavy, rusted chain looped through the iron handles. She tugged. The hinges groaned but opened only an inch. Not a large enough space for a child to crawl through. But what if she'd found another way inside?

"These were locked exactly this way?"

He nodded. "Yeah. And the well inside was boarded off back in the eighties. The lock hadn't been tampered with and there's no other way in. Nobody could have gotten in there."

Ryan knew better. *Nothing* was foolproof. She circled the structure, inspecting each wall and every seam in the foundation that might conceal an opening large enough for a child to slip through. Nothing.

She exhaled through her nose and stepped back, eyes sweeping the grounds beyond the brick shell. *Emma. Where are you?*

It could've been pure hope, or a desperate thread of belief, but Ryan didn't feel the girl was dead. Not yet. But if she was alive, then where was she?

"Let's sweep the gardener's shed and then swing back here."

"We'd better hurry, Agent Mills. There aren't many hours of daylight left."

The well house and outbuildings were cleared. Only the forest and lake remained. If Emma had gone toward the water, maybe Lazarus could pick up a final trace. But if she were lost in the woods or dead, then finding her would be more challenging.

Ryan clenched her jaw. Maybe it was time to tell Director Price they couldn't help the agency this time.

CHAPTER 13

Sharp streaks of orange and pink had laced the sky by the time Doc and the others finished their last session. Sunset glowed beyond the treetops, casting the grounds in a dusky blue-gray. It would've been a beautiful evening if not for a missing five-year-old child.

Alive or dead, Emma was out there somewhere.

Ryan stood in the circular driveway, the mansion's long shadow stretching across the expanse of fountains and well-groomed lawns. Coti had disappeared into the house with Dave to begin breaking down the equipment and packing it up again.

Her thumb hovered over the glass screen of her phone, but Ryan couldn't bring herself to dial. Once she made the call, that was it. Agent Finn and his team would return, and the search would resume exactly as they had before.

It felt like walking backwards.

SPECTER was built to solve the unsolvable. Usually, they had a body. Then they would work backward to find the *who* and *how*. But everything about this case was inside out. They knew who, Chad Harrison. But not why? It was the mystery that nobody could solve, and they were running out of time.

Holbrook and Sheriff Watson stepped out of the mansion and made their way down the drive toward Ryan. Every step took her closer to defeat.

Doc placed his hand on her shoulder. "So, are you ready to call it?"

She bit her lip hard enough to push back the sense of overwhelming failure. "I don't want to give up on her."

"We found nothing that they didn't already know," Holbrook said. "Aside from the three rooms upstairs, all we got was static. No leads."

"There has to be something more." Ryan turned toward Matt. "Chad either murdered her and put her somewhere we have yet to find, or she's hiding in the best place *she* could think of. I just . . ."

Her voice trailed off as she gazed out toward the outbuildings, to the servant's house, the stables, the well house. Everything inside her screamed that she was missing something. *Think, Ryan!* A thread she hadn't pulled. A corner she hadn't inspected. Anything before she walked away.

"No." She shoved the phone into her back pocket. "Take me back out to those buildings one more time," she demanded, shooting Watson a determined glance. "And bring your keys. I want to inspect every building personally." Then, she turned toward the house. "Coti, don't load things up yet."

"Okay," Coti shouted from inside the atrium.

The sheriff sighed, grasped the keys from his jacket pocket, and nodded. "Alright." But his words held little conviction. "I'll grab a couple flashlights. It's going to be dark soon."

"Make sure everything is charged up and ready, just in case, Doc. I don't want Lazarus running out of juice at a crucial moment." She walked briskly toward Watson. "Let's go."

As soon as he fished out two flashlights from his SUV, he led the way. Ryan wanted to work backwards this time, a fresh look at everything. One more thorough inspection. She didn't care how long it took—Emma's life depended on them finding her.

At the well house, Watson unlocked the rusted chain, and Ryan immediately yanked the doors open before the links could fall from the latches. Her flashlight cut through the darkness, revealing a space no larger than her dining room. But unlike her home, this place had a cold, ancient stone-mortared well at its center, capped with thick, weather-worn panels nailed into place.

She dropped to a crouch and tried to pry the boards up. They didn't budge, confirming what Watson had said—there was nowhere else to hide.

She stood, brushing off her hands, when she caught movement out of the corner of her eye. Turning sharply, her flashlight darted toward the far wall of the room. She rushed over and found a small break in the brick no bigger than a chicken egg.

"What is it?" Watson joined her.

"Thought I saw something. Must have been an animal." She pointed to the gap.

"Probably a field mouse, Agent Mills."

Ryan rubbed the back of her neck as she followed Watson to the next building. What she'd seen was a lot bigger than a rodent. In fact, she'd swear it was the shadow of a small child, watching them from the darkness.

As much as she didn't want to go into the servant's house, she took in a deep breath and followed the sheriff through the door. While Watson investigated the first floor, Ryan climbed the stairs to the second floor, heading toward the room where she'd seen the woman at the window.

Thump. Thump.

Ryan froze, flashlight gripped in shaking hands. Her pulse pounded wildly in her chest. Taking a few careful steps, the old floorboards groaned beneath her weight. She swept the beam across the floor, illuminating the swirling dust.

Thump.

"Emma?" she called softly. "I'm Agent Mills with the FBI. If you're hurt, call out, or make a noise. Sheriff Watson is here with me."

Ryan moved slowly, her breath shallow. As she crossed the threshold of the first room, a chill swept across her skin. Yet, the mini-Lazarus watch remained silent.

The room was Spartan, containing only an antique four-poster bed and a two-drawer dresser.

No buzzing.

No blood.

No Puritan woman lingering in the shadows.

She crossed to the window, pulling back the lace curtain. Outside, the lake and well house faded from view, swallowed by the last trace of sunlight slipping below the horizon.

A breeze stirred the trees, and the old house creaked in response.

Thump. Thump.

Soft. Distant. Somewhere above her.

She stood still, head lifted toward the ceiling. Listening. The hairs on her arms prickled, and she shivered. Old houses *were* prone to drafts.

Get a grip, Ryan.

Only the wind. Nothing more.

Still, it was enough to make her glance back one last time before heading downstairs.

Despite stacks of boxes and dust-covered furniture, there was no sign of Emma in the servant's house. The gardener's sheds and the greenhouse were just as barren. As Ryan stepped from the greenhouse door, she scanned the grounds, now steeped in inky shadows that crept across the lawns and melted into the edge of the forest. The maple leaves shook in the faint breeze, their brittle sounds like cries in the dark. And a lone sodium lamp glowed above the stable doors, casting a long, unwavering beam across the gravel road.

"Well," Watson said, locking the shed door. "Want to keep going?"

She'd already inspected the stable when daylight made it bright and harmless. Even Watson had searched the building. She turned slowly, hoping to catch a glimpse of anything that could point her in the right direction.

"C'mon," she breathed. "Show me."

The phone in her pocket felt warm, waiting for her call to Agent Finn. She rubbed a hand across her forehead, trying to ease the ache that had started to twist above her eye. There wasn't anywhere else left to look.

A heavy sigh escaped from her chest. "I guess we need to call it."

Watson stepped beside her and directed his flashlight beam across the road leading past the stables and back toward the house. "Everyone's done what they could. Finn plans to dredge the lake tomorrow. And I'm helping them grid-search the woods. If she's out there, we'll find her."

They stepped onto the path. "I'd hoped we could've found *something*. Anything."

Then, Ryan froze when a dark figure emerged from the shadows and slipped into the stables. It could have been her tired eyes playing tricks, but after everything this place had thrown at her today, she didn't dare dismiss it.

"Did you see that?" Watson said, grabbing her arm.

That was all the confirmation she needed. "Yeah. Someone went into the stables."

"Is that one of your guys?"

"I don't think so. There's no reason for them to come back here."

"Okay," he whispered. Everything about him shifted. His gaze locked forward—steady and sharp—shoulders braced as he reached for the firearm at his belt. Ryan mirrored his movements, drawing her weapon and aligning it with the flashlight in her other hand.

Their eyes met.

She gave a nod, and he returned it.

Ryan moved first, stepping into the shadows that stretched along the stable wall. The sheriff followed close behind as they approached the side wall and crouched below the level of windows. The grounds had fallen eerily still except for the breeze threading through the trees.

No sound came from inside the building.

No creaking floorboards. No footsteps. No breathing.

Nothing.

With her back pressed against the siding, Ryan edged toward the corner of the building where bright light filled the space beyond. She barely heard Watson's movements and cast a quick glance over her shoulder to confirm he was still there. He was. Focused and ready.

Another nod passed between them.

Her grip tightened around the gun, one finger along the frame above the trigger. One final breath and she surged forward, stepping into the light.

"This is Special Agent Mills with the FBI," she called out. "You're trespassing on private property. Come out now."

In open space beyond the gaping doors lay a disquieting abyss—colorless and dead. If Watson hadn't seen it too, she might be questioning what she'd witnessed.

"Come out with your hands up," she commanded, louder this time. The steel in her voice didn't mask the tension burning in her arms as white-knuckled fingers tightened around her weapon.

Still no answer.

A sharp *ping* pierced the growing night. The sodium lamp blinked, then went out, plunging them into darkness.

Ryan gasped at the sudden absence of light. The stable door stood open, yawning like the mouth of a shark. But she didn't move. Not until her watch started to frantically buzz against her wrist.

That small breath stuck in her chest felt like a razor blade. She tilted her wrist enough to see the watch's strobing lights as the vibration shook against her wrist. A ring of red flashed around the edges—except the flashing green indicator pointing directly into the depths of the stable.

This is all wrong. It has to be. Not again.

She swallowed hard and lifted her right heel enough to signal Watson what she was about to do. Then she stepped forward, turning to face the gaping darkness.

The flashlight beam barely reached a quarter of the length of the walkway, which was hemmed in by rows of empty stalls on either side.

"Come out now," she shouted into the dark.

The flashlight beam scanned across the building, but the walkway appeared empty. The light barely rose to the arching ceiling high above, like a vaulted cathedral that stretched forth and plunged deep into the blackness, with rows of horse stalls for pews. Every stall door stood almost five feet high—tall enough to conceal a full-grown adult.

As Ryan moved, sweeping her light across the room, the floor-to-ceiling posts created shadows that seemed to slither across the walls.

If this had been one of her people, they would have acknowledged her the moment she called out. The longer the silence, the more her skin crawled. And the pulsing on her wrist didn't help to ease her nerves—it stung like a live wire.

She lowered her voice, barely above a breath. "I'm going in."

"I've got your back," Watson whispered, gun and flashlight ready.

She stepped forward, plunging deeper into the barn, as shadows clawed at the edge of her beam. Watson followed behind her, staying to her left. As she scanned the first stall on the right, he mirrored her movement on the left.

"I'm telling you again," she called out. "I am Special Agent Mills with the FBI. Declare yourself."

Only their muffled footsteps answered. When light caught nothing but a carpet of golden hay scattered on the floor, she moved to the next stall.

The watch buzzed faster than she'd ever felt before. The green LED light flashed wildly, the bar furiously pointing toward the far end of the stable. As Ryan moved toward the inky abyss, the bulb in her flashlight suddenly exploded.

"Ahh!" Startled, she dropped her flashlight, and the darkness swallowed her.

"Mills!" Watson called, sweeping his beam in her direction, but it barely penetrated the void.

She turned toward his voice—

And then she heard it.

A low growl vibrated through the floor. Like distant thunder in the earth and on the horizon, but it emanated from *inside* the building, growing upon itself until she felt it deep in her chest. This was no human.

And it hadn't followed them. It had *lured* them here.

The sound thickened, pressing into her ribs, crawling into every joint in her body, until the watch buzz became indistinguishable from the hum in her bones.

Then, something moved.

Almost imperceptible. It shifted in the darkness, a mass, darker than the shadows. The creature crawled along the back wall—its breath a foul stench—hot and rotting. Ryan couldn't see it, but she could *feel* it—its size, its awareness . . . its rage.

Watson's footsteps stirred behind her, and she threw out her arm, fingers splayed to stop him.

He froze, flashlight trained on her back. "What is it?" he whispered. "Do you see someone?"

Ryan's breath was quick and shallow, her legs refusing to move.

The thing shifted again.

Every cell in her body sensed it. She again willed her legs to move away, but they wouldn't respond. Ryan steadied her breath, hoping to be as quiet as possible—to become as invisible as possible. Maybe, if neither of them moved, it would leave them alone.

But this was no black bear or a trapped mountain lion. This was something else entirely. This creature wasn't *of this* world.

Ryan flicked her hand toward Watson, and the sound of his slow retreat bounded against the walls. But that was enough to get its attention. The thing huffed again, and this time, a violent gust roared down the aisle like a freight train. Ryan stumbled as it barreled past, catching Watson full-force and lifting him off his feet. He flew backward through the open stable doors, hitting the lawn with a heavy thud. His flashlight clattered to the floor and blinked out.

The shock snapped Ryan into action. She turned and ran, focusing on the distant lights of the mansion through the open doors. Four seconds. That's all they needed. Just four seconds.

Cold night air that drifted into the stable hit her face. She gasped for each breath.

Three seconds.

She could make it. Two seconds. Almost there—

Something grasped her ankle, pulling her legs out from under her. Ryan slammed chest-first onto the concrete. Her vision blurred. Watson scrambled to his feet, diving toward the door, his fingers reaching for her outstretched hand.

Ryan screamed as the thing dragged her into the darkness, the sheriff's silhouette dwindling as she was pulled away. The sound tore out of her, raw and uncontained. Her terror echoed through the rafters as she was violently pulled into the creature's lair.

Then—it let go.

She skidded to a stop. Then she sensed the massive form, as shapeless as smoke in the darkness, hovering above her, a freezing cold draining every ounce of warmth from her.

Blood rushed through her ears, unable to drown out the creature's growling, its breathing. It sniffed her hair as a thin, formless tongue brushed against the leather of her boots.

Her numb, trembling hands still gripped the gun.

In one swift movement, she shoved herself upright, flipped over, and fired.

Three times. Four. Five.

The muzzle flash lit the darkness long enough for her to see the thing recoil.

And that was enough.

Scrambling to her feet, Ryan ran for the door. The air burned her lungs as her boots pounded the floor. With every step, she drew closer to the exit.

Watson yelled, hands waving rapidly, urging her onward.

Again, the fresh air filled her lungs. The stable doors loomed ahead. Growling thundered in the air. Talons scraped along the concrete.

It was coming.

Ryan pushed harder as the stench of rot filled her nostrils. Smokey tentacles reached out toward her, growing closer with every second. She didn't dare look back. A chilling thought seeped into her mind.

I am here.

Ryan plunged into the open air and grabbed Watson by the arm, dragging him as she ran past. Together, they sprinted toward the mansion—she couldn't stop—not for a breath or anything.

They bounded up the porch, and Ryan flung the doors open. As Watson stumbled in after her, they both slammed and bolted the door. Then Watson dropped against the door, breathing rapidly. Ryan stood back, eyes wide, expecting the living shadow to seep through the cracks.

"What was that?" Watson gasped, wiping sweat from his brow.

Her lungs burned. Her pulse thundered. But the adrenaline coursing through her veins kept her voice steady.

"We've got more problems than the missing girl."

CHAPTER 14

Ryan had expected the creature to slam against the door or to shatter a window trying to get at them, but nothing happened. Only silence. The chandelier, casting its golden light, felt disturbingly normal—as if the house itself hadn't noticed the monster at its door.

She stood frozen. Each painful breath after another scraped in her ears. Her weapon, trained on the door, burned hot in her hand as trembling fingers wrapped tighter around the grip.

Watson pushed himself away from the door and scrambled to his feet. He must have expected an attack, too, as he stood beside her, gun held in a trembling hand next to his thigh and eyes fixed on the doorknob.

"What did you see?" he whispered, as though something was listening.

That was the problem. She didn't know, and there was no way she was going back outside to find out. Whatever it was, it wasn't human, nor any animal she'd ever encountered.

Footsteps thundered down the staircase. "What on earth . . .?" Holbrook said.

Ryan didn't turn. If the door exploded inward, she wanted to be ready. Coti and Dave emerged from the side hall elevator.

"What's going on?" Dave said, wheeling toward them.

"T-There is something out there," Watson started, his voice

sharp with disbelief. "Something big. In the stables. It grabbed her." He ticked his head toward Ryan.

Holbrook walked across the foyer, eyes fixed on the door as he reached Ryan's side. He didn't ask. One look at her face told him enough.

"I don't know what it was," she whispered. "But it's . . ." she shuddered. "Evil." She turned slightly toward Holbrook, ready to blindly shoot anything that came through the door. "Matt, we need to find that girl or get out of here, now."

"It's not human?" Holbrook kept his voice low.

She shook her head. "No. I'm positive it isn't."

"Then we need to call Agent Finn and get as many people out here as possible. Maybe get animal control."

Ryan exhaled slowly, voice flat. "I don't think *it* cares how many people are out here."

"*It?*"

She refocused on the door. "I don't know what it is, Matt. But I don't recommend giving it more victims to play with."

"Does it has Emma?"

She shrugged. "If it does . . . we may never see her again."

"What's going on?" Coti asked, placing the hard-shell equipment cases onto the floor.

Holbrook turned to her, his jaw tense, hesitation tightening around his frame, a sensation that even Ryan felt crawl across her shoulders. "Everyone. We're done for tonight. Pack up the rest of the equipment as fast as possible."

"Are you sure?" Dave said.

Ryan nodded. "Get it loaded."

Coti stooped to grab the cases again when the chandelier overhead blinked out, as did a host of other lights down both corridors. The glow from the stairwell slowly dimmed and died.

The exterior security lights followed, plunging the mansion into darkness.

Like the stables.

Nobody moved. Ryan heard Watson's breathing halt. That thing could be approaching the mansion right now, and they were trapped inside, waiting for it to attack.

Ryan's fist clenched, and she bolted for the door. They had to get out—*now*. Her fingers found the deadbolt and twisted. She slammed her palm onto the door handle and yanked. The door didn't budge. She pulled harder, putting her entire weight into it.

Watson rushed up, running into Ryan in the darkness. His hand found hers and added his strength to opening the door.

"Ryan," Coti shouted, "w-what's going on?"

"We have to get out of here." She raised a foot against the doorframe and pulled with the sheriff.

"Why?"

Ryan let go, breath ragged, and scanned the atrium. There had to be another way. If they couldn't get out through the door, then they'd go through a window. While Watson continued to yank at the door, she darted toward the far side of the room where an antique wooden chair rested against the wall. Grabbing it with both hands, she held it like a battering ram and stepped up to the window.

Watson glanced at her, and she expected him to object, given the historic nature of the house and that particular chair, but he said nothing. The whites of his eyes shone in the faint moonlight that filtered through the window's curtains.

She twisted her torso and swung hard, expecting the glass to shatter. Instead, the chair ricocheted back, sending painful shockwaves radiating up her arms and nearly knocking her off her feet.

The glass didn't break or crack. It didn't even *vibrate*. It was like hitting reinforced, bulletproof lead panels. A place like this shouldn't have glass this strong. Not unless—

Gritting her teeth, she wrapped her hands around the chair again and ran full force toward the windowpane, delivering a more powerful swing. The legs of the antique chair shattered on impact, sending shards of wood and splinters back toward her.

But the glass remained flawless.

"What the hell?" Watson said. "That glass is original from when this place was first built. A strong wind could break it." He faced the glass, shoulders squared, and raised his right arm.

In that second, Ryan knew what he was about to do. He still had the gun in his hand, and now it aimed directly at the glass that wouldn't break.

"Wait—" she shouted as the gun fired.

Ryan lunged, tackling Colter before the bullet ricocheted and buried itself in the wall plaster behind them.

Watson blinked, stunned. "I don't understand."

"Neither do I," Ryan said, pushing upright from where she'd knocked him to the floor. "But I don't think we can leave."

She stood and helped Watson to his feet. Although the shot had left a ringing in her ears, everything else had fallen silent. They might be trapped *in* the house, but at least that thing hadn't followed them. As hard as it was for her to understand, maybe this was the mansion's way of protecting them.

At least, that's what she hoped.

The house already held more than anyone else could see. And perhaps, even more than *she* was aware of. Well, if they couldn't get out, maybe somebody could break in. She pulled her phone from her pocket and powered up the screen. The glow illuminated her face, a bright contrast to the dark of the room.

Then her heart fell. No Signal.

Watson must have noticed the defeat in her eyes. "You've got to be kidding me. Nothing?"

She shook her head.

He sighed. "And my radio's in the car."

"Will someone please explain what the hell is going on?" Coti called from the dark.

"I'd like to know the same thing," Watson said as he holstered his weapon.

So much for classified. Ryan couldn't keep him in the dark—not anymore. They were all in this now, whether they liked it or not. And, if they were all stuck here, they might as well keep working. Maybe the house would reveal more—about Emma or about whatever was out in the stables.

All of their equipment was self-powered. They could work until morning if they had to, especially with the additional battery packs in the computer cases.

Ryan pocketed her phone. It was useless anyway. "Sheriff—"

"We're all stuck here," he said, cutting her off with a tired smile. "Call me Colter."

"Okay," she nodded. "Earlier, you said this entire place was haunted."

His brows knit together. "Yeah, but that was. . . Wait. Are you serious?"

"Absolutely."

Colter glanced at the others, as if waiting for someone to laugh and let him in on the joke. Then he finally looked back at Ryan. "Those are only stories."

"You said it yourself; you witnessed things when working as a tour guide. Do you believe this place is haunted?"

He hesitated and glanced at the others again. "What does that have to do with Emma?"

"Because we are not your run-of-the-mill crime scene analysts."

Holbrook stepped in. "We're part of a classified division of the FBI—the Society for Paranormal Evaluation, Classification, Training, Experimentation, and Research. SPECTER. We were sent here to do what we do best—to find that little girl."

"Wait," Colter blinked. "Are you guys like ghost hunters? You're looking for ghosts?"

"No," Ryan said. "Not exactly."

"We can evaluate for energy left behind when someone dies," Dave said, rolling. "It leaves an imprint, a recording, that we can analyze."

"So, not ghosts," Colter repeated, but the lines around his eyes indicated that he didn't believe them.

"Not in the classical or literary sense of the word," Coti added.

But Ryan glanced at Holbrook, who was already looking at her. They shared the weight of what the others didn't know. These *were* the ghosts of the dead, and some of them could communicate with her. Dave and Coti were unaware of the experiment they'd conducted, where Ryan walked into the power that Lazarus had created and had actually communicated with the victims of The Man Who Wasn't There. They didn't know that she could see them, re-live their final moments of life in her mind as she evaluated the crime scenes.

She turned back to Colter. "We were sent here to evaluate the murder scenes. Our director was hoping we could find something that would lead us to Emma. But so far, we've seen nothing."

"So let's keep looking," Holbrook said. "There are over two hundred rooms in this place. Maybe there's something the other agents may have missed."

Colter's gaze remained unchanged. Ryan knew that look too well. She'd worn it herself not so long ago, when first joining the team. Skepticism laced every crease in his face as it had for her until she witnessed the images that Lazarus offered. Until she watched the confused face of a dead woman rise from a still corpse.

Only, Colter would never hear the voices like she did. Nor the whispers they so desperately want to share. If the spirits in this house *did* know what happened to Emma, now was the time to use Lazarus—to dive deep and draw them out of the shadows.

CHAPTER 15

"Tell me everything you know about the hauntings," Ryan said.

Colter glanced to the empty corner of the room and rested his hands on the edge of his jeans. "Let me think; it's been a while." He rubbed the back of his neck. "The house was originally the Treadwell Mansion, named after George and Gloria Treadwell, built in 1889. But, like I told you earlier, the land was already occupied. Some structures date back to the early 1700s. I mentioned the girl in the servant's house."

"The one who killed herself?" Ryan said.

"Yeah."

"How did she die?" Ryan asked.

"Hanging, I think. At least that's what we were told to say during the haunted tour nights."

"Who else?" Ryan pressed.

Colter's brow creased as he sifted through memory. "The Treadwells both died here. Gloria killed herself in the third-floor bathtub—cut her wrists. I know that one is true. I saw the newspaper article myself. And George shot himself during the 1929 Great Depression. I guess they lost a lot in the stock market crash."

"Where did he shoot himself?"

"The conservatory," he said, tipping his head toward the corridor to his left.

During the morning tour, Colter had taken her through most of the critical locations in the mansion, including the conservatory—a vast glass structure flanking the pool complex, and caged in ornate, wrought ironwork and paned in glass. The humidity of the conservatory was likely oppressive in the heat of the day, but the enormous greenery that grew in there provided enough shade to make it the perfect quiet escape.

And it was also the perfect place to die, at least for Mr. Treadwell.

"Excuse me," Coti broke in. "Is *anybody* going to explain why this is important? Or why we can't get out of here?"

Ryan turned, locking eyes with her friend. "I'm working on it," she said softly. "I promise. But, right now, I'm not sure yet. Okay?"

Coti and Dave nodded.

Thankful for their trust, Ryan returned to the task. She had a lot of possible theories, but none could explain that *thing* in the stables. Yet, the more she tried to reason it out, the more it felt . . . familiar. A chill trickled along her spine. The same sensation she had before stepping into the stable. Instinctive. As if her body *knew* what was in there. Because she had *met* it before.

Ryan's eyes flashed wide. "Oh!" She remembered. The watch on her wrist had warned her both times when she needed to be alert. The second time was in the stable. But the first time was at the police station of Currant Falls when she sat across the table from Chad Harrison. That cold, empty darkness in his eyes. A shadow without weight or name.

Like the thing in the stables.

"I . . . have an idea," she said slowly. It was only partial, but the moment she connected with Chad's interrogation, everything started to make sense.

"We're going to take Lazarus to each of these rooms Colter mentioned. Then, we'll expand our search."

"Why?" Dave asked. "We're not investigating those deaths."

"Because Emma wasn't present in rooms where her family died. We know that. But this place—" she swept her gaze across the room "—has *other* witnesses." Her glance met Holbrook's, and they exchanged the same thought: it was time to show them exactly what she was capable of.

"So," Dave said, the word escaping slowly from his lips, "you're saying you believe this place is haunted, and that will somehow help us."

"That is precisely what she is saying." Holbrook's English accent sharpened with each word, and he stood taller, hands stuffed into his pockets. "What you do not know is that Mills and I have been conducting experiments, particularly with the case from last year."

As their eyes adjusted to the semi-darkness, Coti and Dave glanced at each other with the same understanding. They knew exactly which case he meant. The one that nearly tore them apart. The one that almost killed Coti and Ryan, and the one that changed them forever. The one that revealed their department director, Special Agent Sam Masters, as *The Man Who Wasn't There*.

"Those experiments aided in solving that case," Holbrook continued. "And they proved Lazarus is capable of far more than we ever thought possible."

"I'm sorry," Colter said. "Lazarus? Like the dude from the Bible?"

Ryan nodded at him. "Yeah, kind of like that."

She turned to the others. "I think we should try doing the same thing we did last year. Maybe I can get something from the others that are still here."

"The others?" Coti's voice dropped almost to a whisper.

Ryan nodded. "The ghosts of Treadwell mansion."

In the dark, it was impossible to read their faces. Maybe they believed her. Maybe they didn't. All it would take was one try with Lazarus to convince them. Ghost stories were easy to dismiss until they weren't stories anymore.

At least Holbrook understood what the other didn't: when she stepped into Lazarus's electromagnetic field, she crossed into a world in stasis—some might call it Purgatory—where the dead waited for someone to hear their story. She'd spoken with her deceased sister, as well as others. Perhaps it could work in finding a missing child.

Coti clapped her hands, the sound echoing through the atrium. "Alright, then let's get to work. Where do you want to start?"

"The third-floor bathroom," Ryan said, turning to Colter. "Lead the way."

"What about him?" Colter gestured, pointing to Dave. "Power's out, and so is the elevator."

Coti grinned. "We've done this a thousand times. There's enough of us to get him up there, if he even allows us to help him. He's got arms like a gorilla and usually crawls up himself."

"That's right, I do." Dave flexed an arm dramatically.

"C'mon King Kong. Up you go."

"Aye, aye, Captain." Dave gave Holbrook a quick salute and wheeled to the base of the stairs. As Coti predicted, he moved smoothly from the chair to the steps and started climbing at a quick pace. Holbrook folded the chair and carried it alongside Coti, who hoisted the equipment cases with practiced ease.

Colter lingered at Ryan's side. "Are you going to tell them what really happened in the stables?"

"Not yet," she murmured. "I don't want to scare them."

"And what about me? Are you going to tell *me*?"

A dry knot formed in her throat. "I honestly don't know what it was. Something big and dark and horrible. And I think it's connected to what happened to the Harrisons."

He shot a glance up the staircase. "Is it one of your ghosts?"

"I don't think so. I think it's much worse. I've never seen anything like it."

A sigh fell from his lips. "Well, that's reassuring." He turned and started up after the others.

Ryan's legs felt like two stumps that would never move again. She'd been ready to follow, but Colter's question unearthed the thing that lingered at the edges of her mind. That *thing*—whether it could enter the house or not—had already touched her life. And everything in her screamed it was connected to Chad Harrison.

It hadn't merely influenced him. Maybe, it had *used* him.

And the house, locking its doors, sealing its windows—was it protecting them? Or trapping inside? She didn't know. Perhaps Lazarus *was* the only key she had to finding that answer.

The atrium sank deeper into darkness, swallowing the light filtering through the windows. Ryan was alone with that gaping black coming from all sides, like it did every night when she turned off her bedroom lights. Only this time, she couldn't turn them back on to keep those memories away. Every flicker of moonlight through the windows reflected on something inside. The shadows were long in places. Too long.

Shapes bled along the walls, forming a tall silhouette that lingered beside the stair banister. Always a man. Always watching.

It was Sam. Waiting to come back. Like he was after Lexi died. Like he'd been the night she first heard the poem.

Yesterday, upon the stair . . .

Ryan's ribs tightened, breath quickening as that first stab of panic struck. Pressure flooded into her chest like rising water.

I saw a man who wasn't there.

The FBI therapist's instructions were to center herself during moments when fear tried to take over, but damn, that was hard to do without lights. There was nothing but darkness.

She needed to breathe. It was harder now. No lights. No safe edges. Elongated shadows crept across the ascending staircase. Ryan gripped the wooden rail. Hand muscles locked.

He wasn't there again today . . .

She closed her eyes. *It's not real. It's not real.* She'd shot Sam in the head. He was never coming back.

Oh, how I wish he'd go away.

Panic clawed at her, and the air wouldn't fill her lungs fast enough.

"Are you coming?" Holbrook's voice called from the second-floor landing.

His voice broke the vice holding her. Air rushed into her lungs. The tightness released.

"It's okay," she muttered. "You'll be okay."

Despite her trembling, she drew in a steady breath, squared her shoulders, and stepped forward.

"I'll be right up."

The shadows on the stairs were just that. Shadows, and nothing more. They didn't move. They didn't breathe. They didn't *watch.*

That shadow was still outside.

For now.

CHAPTER 16

Most bathrooms don't simultaneously inspire a sense of dread and awe, but this one did. Probably because they knew a suicide had occurred here more than a century ago. Or perhaps it was something deeper. Ryan entered a room larger than her bedroom back home. Three large, curtained windows looked out over the grounds, allowing enough moonlight to illuminate a claw-foot bathtub centered atop a bed of pristine, white tiles.

At the far end of the room stood a pedestal sink, its silver handles and faucet curving over the wide porcelain basin. Above it hung a large silver mirror adorned in a gilded frame. Even the commode was a sterile white porcelain complete with a high-mounted Victorian-style tank and a silver chain.

"Well, if you want to find a ghost," Colter said, breaking the silence, "this is probably the best place to start. Everything in this room is original from the day the mansion was built. And that tub was cut from a single slab of marble, FYI."

Ryan said nothing. She already knew what had happened. Gloria Treadwell had drawn a razor across her wrists and bled out into a tub full of water. In the pale blue moonlight, only Ryan saw the water, dark as oil. Droplets of blood glistened on the tiles below, a trail leading to a straight razor on the floor, its blade coated in a black slick of blood. She closed her eyes, trying to push the image from her mind.

"The room's big enough to set everything up," Coti said. "Good thing we hadn't packed anything in the vehicle; it's all down the hall. I'll start setting up."

When Ryan opened her eyes again, the blood-stained water was gone. The razor had disappeared, leaving a clean, white tile floor. She stepped around the tub, examining the sink. The basin was dry and spotless. Everything exactly as it was when they first walked into the room.

When everything was assembled, Dave powered up the computer with Holbrook standing nearby, arms crossed.

"Start with the lowest settings, Dave," he said. "We'll build up the EMF gradually."

Coti passed out the viewing glasses needed to view the Lazarus images, but Ryan shook her head.

"I won't need them, not where I'm going."

Coti looked toward Holbrook, her brow furrowed.

Holbrook nodded. He then held out one open palm toward the machine mounted on a tripod in the center of the bathroom. "Sheriff, meet Lazarus."

Ryan did her best to ignore them as she stepped beyond the table and approached the device. She'd only done this a couple of times, and both left her with a pounding headache and a bloody nose. At least both forays into Purgatory had started with tangible crime scene evidence to anchor her. This room held only a story. Hopefully, that would be enough.

Dave glanced up. "We're ready to fire up. Mills, you've gotta move—you're standing right in the Lazarus field."

Holbrook intervened. "This is the experiment we told you about. Let it play out."

"But that level of EMF could be dangerous," Dave said, pushing up his glasses.

"I'm aware," Ryan said, her voice calm.

"Wait," Dave said. "You mean you actually sit inside the electromagnetic zone?"

Ryan's eyebrows rose as she gave him a wry nod. "That's how it works, Wheels."

Without another word, she sat cross-legged on the floor, in the center of the grid zone. Cold tiles chilled through her slacks as her hands rested on her knees.

"As always," Holbrook said gently, "call out if you need help."

She nodded. He said that both times they had done it before, but it didn't really help much.

"Are you sure about this, boss?" Dave asked, glancing up one last time at Holbrook.

"Absolutely."

Dave cleared his throat. "Okay. Powering up." His fingers raced across the keyboard and then, with one final keystroke, the four cameras blinked to life. Another tap of the keys and a low hum vibrated from the Lazarus unit as it rose on a pole in the center of the tripod. The blue laser grid fanned out across the room as a soft whirring sound emanated from within the machine.

Ryan closed her eyes. The hum crawled over her skin, raising goosebumps in its wake. It sank deep into her bones, leaving a cadence like a metronome in her head, fast and steady. A sudden flash of light burst around her, bright enough to see through closed eyelids. Its residue felt like an impact tremor that took her breath away. When she finally inhaled again, the air was cold. Icy. Her eyes flew open.

The bathroom was no longer plunged into midnight darkness. The warm glow from a single candle resting on the tile floor at the end of the bathtub flickered softly, causing the shadows to dance around the empty room. No Lazarus. No team. Just her.

Then the door creaked open, and a woman entered. Barefoot, silent. Ryan stood quickly and stepped back against the sink. The figure moved into the halo of candlelight, illuminating the faint details of her pale skin. A silky, cream-colored slip hung loosely from bony shoulders. Black hair in a bob cut framed a face streaked with tears and mascara. A smear of red lipstick marred the corner of her trembling mouth as a shuddered breath escaped her lips, fragile and broken.

She sat on the edge of the tub and turned the knob until water streamed from the tap into the marble basin. As the tub filled, her other hand moved into the light, and Ryan caught the glint of a straight razor, closed within the sheath.

The woman sobbed again, the black drops of tears and mascara falling into the growing pool of water.

This was exactly what Ryan had hoped to find. Not the act, but enough residual energy for her to be here. She only hoped it was enough for Lazarus to record. She swallowed, then forced out the words in barely more than a whisper.

"Gloria Treadwell?"

The woman didn't look up but continued to swirl her fingers in the tub of water.

"Mrs. Treadwell, can you hear me?"

"I will not stop, if that's what you want," Gloria murmured, gazing at her distorted reflection in the water.

She *could* hear her. Perhaps even see her standing there. Ryan took a step closer. What could Gloria think of this strange figure that appeared in her washroom, watching her as she cried?

"Gloria, I need your help."

The woman reached forward and shut off the faucet. The

final drips fell into the pool. Her sobs returned, and her shoulders shuddered.

"I never wanted to do this," she whispered. "But I had no choice."

"Gloria—Mrs. Treadwell . . ."

"Don't call me that!" she snapped, her eyes meeting Ryan's. "That makes me sound like an old hag."

"I'm sorry." Ryan softened her tone. "Gloria, please. I'm looking for a little girl that lives here: Emma Harrison. Have you seen her?"

Gloria turned away and gazed back into the water. She swung her left leg into the pool and then her right.

"I have no more children here," she sobbed. "They've all left me."

The woman slid into the water, her gown floating for a moment before slipping beneath the surface. Long, pale arms draped over the sides of the marble tub as water lapped at her shoulders.

Ryan stepped closer. "Not *your* children, Gloria. Another child."

"They have all left me." She raised the straight razor and opened the sheath.

"Please, Gloria," Ryan said, rushing to the edge of the tub. Her hand gripped the woman's wrist, halting the blade's descent. The woman's eyes shot toward her, pupils black in the flickering light.

The watch on Ryan's wrist buzzed violently enough to make her grip release. The vibration shot through her bones, and she staggered back. Gloria's eyes followed Ryan as she moved away. Then, the buzzing stopped.

"I told you, I didn't want to do this," Gloria said. The razor still hovered above the water. "It made me have those thoughts. They weren't my own."

"What made you do it?"

Beyond the candlelight, a dark mist coalesced at the edge of the doorway and curled around the frame. Then, it settled on the white tiles and, like slow-moving ink in water, it crept over the floor in long, filmy tentacles until it swirled at the base of the tub. Then it snaked up the sides and over the lip, wrapping around Gloria's damp shoulders. She didn't seem to notice, and if she did, she paid it no attention. The tentacles thinned into black, misty vines that coiled up her neck, around her ears, and toward her face.

Gloria didn't flinch. Didn't cry out.

The black mist plunged into her eyes, ears, nostrils, and mouth, and the woman only sighed as if welcoming it.

Before Ryan could intervene, Gloria drew the razor across her wrist with the ease of a violin bow. A fine line of red bloomed in the water. With trembling fingers, she gripped the razor and slid her other wrist across the blade. Those same trembling fingers tipped the razor over the lip of the tub, and it clattered to the floor as droplets of blood dripped from her fingertips. The woman rested her head back against the marble, her arms slipping into the pool as the blood pulsated out of her body.

Gloria Treadwell had taken her life—or so it would seem. *The thoughts weren't her own.* The thing that slithered into her might have been the thing in the stables.

There was no helping Gloria. This was a hundred-year-old tragedy, an imprint of what had happened then. But its playback had given Ryan more than expected.

She turned toward the open door. The black mist had come from the corridor. Stepping into the hallway, out of the light provided by the candle, Ryan plunged into shadow. The corridor looked almost the same as when she entered Lazarus. The same dark red carpets stretched down each hallway. The same lacy curtains hung over each window.

The farther she moved away from the bathroom, the less she could see down the corridor. Even the light from the windows stopped well before the end of the hall, leaving it an absolute void.

She headed toward the bedroom where the Harrisons died. Maybe there was something in Purgatory waiting within that room. Something with answers.

"You do not want to go that way," a voice warned.

Startled, she turned to see a familiar face. The thin, gaunt figure dressed in a black suit, very much like a tuxedo. A clean white towel was draped over an arm held at an angle against the torso. It was the same man she'd seen on the third floor earlier. The same man who had vanished.

"Who are you?" she said, trying to catch her breath.

"Gustav. The butler." He dipped into a slight bow. His accent, faintly German, carried a tone of old-world refinement.

"Why shouldn't I go that way?" Ryan asked, ticking her head down the corridor.

His head tilted as he glanced down the hallway behind her. "There is nothing but the worst thoughts of mankind down there. Anger. Rage. You won't find what you seek."

Something had kept his spirit in this house all these years. "Is that what you found down there?"

A glint of a smile appeared on his thin lips. "I never go down there, but others have."

"Gustav, have you seen a little girl around here? Emma Harrison?"

The smile faded. "I have seen many children come and go. Dreadful business, what happened down there." His gaze again drifted down the hall. "But she is not there."

"So, you *do* know where she is." Ryan's heart rate increased.

His head turned to gaze back at the staircase. "Duty calls, miss. I appear to have been remiss in my services. The master of the house will not be pleased."

"Gustav . . . Wait!"

He turned away, and her voice stopped short in her throat. A gaping gunshot wound in the back of his head. Splayed open edges. Blood. Bits of bone and brain dangling in his graying hair. *Close-range rifle fire.* Gustav continued down the corridor and disappeared down the stairwell as if he had no idea it was there.

Ryan waited a few moments, hoping that Gustav would reappear. Slowly, she turned back toward the long hallway and stared at the stagnant blackness. The hairs on her arms prickled, and then the shadow began to shift like wind-blown sand. Was this the tentacled, black thing that had crept into the bathroom? That hid in the stables, waiting to take something, anything?

"What are you?" she called out, but it only continued to shift and curl in the shadows.

Ryan moved down the corridor, each step heavier than the last, like slogging through thick mud. The closer she got, the more it undulated—like black oil in water. The odor of sulfur and ash drifted across the space toward her. Prickled bumps rose across her arms at its low chittering. By the time she reached the Harrisons' bedroom door, the dark figure had taken shape. A head, shoulders, torso, and legs. A human form. It took one step forward, enough for the light to barely reach the tip of its feet. But it was enough for Ryan to make out its features.

Especially the eyes, with a silver flash like the eyes of a wild animal—a predator. She had seen that in only one other person before.

"Chad? Chad Harrison?" she whispered.

The figure stepped forward, letting the moonlight fall across him. The man wasn't Chad. He stood there, no longer a dark figure cast in shadows, but flesh and bone. Short, sandy-blonde hair, cut short. Broad shoulders and chest were decorated with tattoos. And his bare muscular torso revealed the ink of a skull—a skull with emerald-green eyes that peeked just above the waistline.

No! It's impossible.

Ryan's lungs seized. Her vision blurred. With each passing second, she fought for breath.

Sam. Sam Masters.

She closed her eyes. *No. No. It can't be.* She shot him, more than once. Her eyelids flew open. "You're dead. You aren't real!"

Her eyes flew open to see him still standing there. Trembling fingers found the wall, and she stepped back. That was the moment he broke into a sprint toward her.

Ryan turned and bolted toward the bathroom, his footsteps thundering behind her. The candlelight glow was a faint beacon, urging her on. Reaching the doorframe, she pulled herself inside, slamming the door shut.

A crash hit the other side. The knob twisted as she flipped the lock.

This can't be happening.

She backed into the sink and turned to face herself in the mirror. Her reflection stared back—wild-eyed and pale. Behind her, the door rattled on its hinges, the knob twisting incessantly.

"Let me in, Ryan," it seethed in Sam's voice, low and brutal.

"Get me out of here!" she screamed. "Holbrook—anyone!"

The door rattled again, then a heavy thud hit the center of

it. The wood panels creaked and split in the center. *He's breaking through!*

"Ryan," he growled. "You can't hide from me."

She tore her gaze away from the reflection of the door and toward her face. "GET ME OUT OF HERE!" Her fists flew, smashing into the mirror. The glass splintered into a thousand jagged shards, fracturing her reflection.

She heard the door shatter.

And the scream that followed was hers.

CHAPTER 17

The last syllable of her scream barely left her throat before she fell back, arms and legs outstretched, into Holbrook's arms. She was still sitting on the cold tile floor, but the sound of the mirror cracking still echoed in her ears. The candlelight had vanished, replaced by the digital glow of indicator lights from the cameras and Dave's monitor.

"I have you," Holbrook whispered, pulling her against his chest.

The room plunged into darkness, and there wasn't enough air to fill her lungs as they fought for air. Her eyes frantically searched the corners for any lingering signs of Sam. Then Ryan twisted in Holbrook's grip, eyes locking on the door.

It stood wide open.

"What happened in there?" Coti asked from behind the table of computers.

"He was there," Ryan choked out. She broke Holbrook's grasp and scrambled to her feet, stumbling toward the doorway. The corridor beyond lay in shadow, as it had in Purgatory. No figures lingered. No Sam. Only five of them were in the room.

She turned back and caught her reflection in the mirror. But it was fractured. Glass had been shattered in a spiderweb of concentric circles and jagged lines from a central impact. But she'd shattered it in Purgatory. Not here. So, how had the mirror broken in this reality?

"Damn," Cotler muttered, stumbling back until his shoulders hit the wall. He yanked off the viewing glasses. "What the hell did I just see?"

"Did you do that?" Holbrook said, nodding to the mirror.

"I . . . I think I did."

Coti and Dave still stared at her, eyes wide, speechless.

"Was that Gloria Treadwell?" Colter asked, his voice unsteady as he looked toward the empty bathtub.

"Did you record it?" Ryan asked, her hands still grasping the doorframe with white knuckles.

Dave nodded. "We saw her—in the bathtub. We saw everything."

"All of it? Even the black mist?"

Dave blinked. "What mist?"

Holbrook stepped closer. "Ryan, what did you see in there?"

It sounded insane, even to her. Sam couldn't be in there. He had no connection with this house. He wasn't one of the lingering spirits that roamed its hallways.

Still, her gaze drifted down the hall to the farthest end where the moonlight never reached. A seemingly benign darkness. The same place where the mist had first appeared. Where she knew the shadow still lingered.

"Ryan?" Holbrook's tone was gentle, edged with concern.

She didn't have the answers they needed, and the increasing tightening in her chest twisted deeper, telling her that she needed to get away. Now. A panic attack in front of her team would only worry them further. She pushed off the doorframe and plunged into the corridor toward the stairwell. Going even deeper into the dark. It didn't matter. She reached the banister and gripped it tight with both hands.

The need to center herself overwhelmed everything else.

Five things you can feel. The therapist's voice rang in her head. Her fingertips curled around the firm wood of the banister. She bent over, pressing her forehead to the railing.

Wood. Cold, polished wood.

A tooth bit down slightly onto her lip. *Pain. That's three. Now two more.*

"Are you okay?" Holbrook spoke. His voice had lowered enough that the others couldn't hear them.

Of course. She hadn't gotten away from him after all.

"I don't know, Matt."

He crouched beside her, trying to meet her eyes. "Please let me help you. Tell me what you saw."

Four things you can see . . . or, more accurately, what she'd *seen.*

She steadied her breathing enough to speak. "Gloria Treadwell was there. I spoke to her."

"We saw the replay of her suicide."

Ryan shook her head. "There was something else. I think something made her do it. It's part of this house, or maybe the land. I don't know."

"How do you know that?"

She sat down, pressing her back against the railing. "I saw something in the stables, earlier when I did the final walk-through with Watson. It was massive. Dark. Definitely not human. It . . . it grabbed me and pulled me toward it. I-I have no idea what it was."

Matt went quiet before he sat beside her. "But definitely paranormal?"

She hadn't thought of it that way until now, but it made sense. "Yeah."

"Can you describe it?"

"Black mist that folds in on itself, but not mist sometimes. It had limbs and could become solid, like when it grabbed me."

"And you saw it again, just now? When you spirit walked?"

Ryan squinted at him. "Spirit walked?"

He grinned faintly. "That's what I'm calling it. We could call it something else. Ghost jumping?"

"I like spirit walk better." For the first time since her return, the pressure in her chest loosened. "Yeah, I saw it in there, Doc. It entered Gloria—infected her somehow. I think it made her do what she did. I saw it *bleed* into her, if that makes any sense."

Holbrook grew silent again, something he always did when he was in deep thought, choosing his words carefully. "I don't wish to alarm you . . . but I believe that we are dealing with a non-human entity."

"Non-human?" She's sensed it before, but prayed she was wrong.

He glanced back down the hallway to the bathroom door, where the others still lingered. "Non-human entities can come in a variety of forms." He dropped his voice even lower. "Not an animal. Not a human spirit. I believe this could be something much older. Possibly an elemental or a demon."

"A demon?" she said with a short, nervous laugh. "Like in *The Exorcist*?"

"You doubt the existence of demons," Holbrook said gently, "after everything you've seen?"

Doc made a good point. Ryan had walked among spirits, spoken to them more than once. And something had grabbed her. Something had influenced Gloria Treadwell to take her own life. And in Purgatory, it had done something else—something much worse.

"Believe it or not," he continued, "that thing has probably been on this land long before the first structures were built."

"Could it make itself look like someone you know?" Ryan asked.

Holbrook nodded. "Yes. There's significant documentation of demon mimicry, especially in hauntings. It often pretends to be a child to gain the trust of the living. Mimics voices. Familiar faces. Why? Did you see someone you recognized in there?"

The answer caught in her throat, as if saying it would make it real. But she knew she had to. "I saw Sam. That thing knows about Sam."

Holbrook's expression darkened. "Well, it *tasted* you, did it not? In the stables? It knows what you fear now."

None of that comforted her, but at least Matt was here. If there was anyone she could trust, it was him.

Inhaling slowly, Holbrook placed a hand on her shoulder. "It *tasted* you, did it not? In the stables. It knows what you fear now, and it's using that to its advantage."

None of this was comforting. At least Matt was there with her. She trusted him. "I don't think any of us are safe, Matt. At first, I thought the house locked us in to keep that thing out, but it's *in* the house. When I was inside Lazarus, it was here. And I don't believe it was merely an imprint from the past. It's hiding—watching. Keeping us trapped with it."

"Makes sense," Holbrook said, nodding. "Entities like that thrive on fear, chaos, despair. Maybe that's the reason so many people have died on this property. It's been feeding for years."

"I think it made Chad Harrison do what he did, and I think a little bit of that thing is still inside of him. I could feel it. And the watch—" she lifted her wrist toward the faint moonlight, "—it sensed it."

"Then it's capable of possession, not just infestation." Matt clapped his hands on his knees and stood. "This is a first for SPECTER."

Ryan stood with him. "I think it's time we told the others. They need to know what we're really up against."

"I couldn't agree more."

CHAPTER 18

Everyone stood in silence as soon as Holbrook finished explaining what had happened. Colter scanned the room, waiting for someone to speak. "I can see why you keep this stuff classified," he said at last. Even in the silvery moonlight, he was paler than usual.

"You can see these things even without Lazarus?" Coti asked, pushing off the wall where she'd been leaning.

"Not like Lazarus does," Ryan said. "But I can see them as though they were right there in front of me."

Coti folded her bare arms over her abdomen. "And this whole time, you didn't say anything."

Ryan lowered her gaze. "I didn't want you to think I was crazy. And an FBI agent isn't supposed to be able to do those things."

"You did learn something, though," Dave said. "From your spirit walk. That thing, whatever it is, had something to do with the Harrisons' murders."

"Maybe. But we're no closer to finding Emma," Ryan said.

"So, we keep trying," Colter interjected.

Something clicked in Ryan's memory—something she'd almost lost in all the chaos of the last hour. "Actually there was something. Colter, do you know of a Gustav who lived here at one time? Shot in the head?"

His expression changed at hearing the name. "Yeah. Gustav Liester. He was the butler when the Barrister family lived here in the 1940's. He was shot in the back of the head by the family's nephew who thought he was a Nazi spy. He wasn't, of course. Just a German immigrant. Wait . . . did you actually see him?"

"A couple of times," Ryan said. "Talked to him, too. Most spirits I meet during a spirit walk don't have much thought or memory beyond their deaths. But he was . . . more aware."

Colter grinned. "I can't believe it. You actually spoke to Gustav. Can I try this Lazarus thing? Do one of those spirit walks you do?"

Holbrook scoffed, giving Colter a slanted look. "This is *not* an amusement ride. We've barely tested the method properly. And frankly, I believe it may only work on someone with Special Agent Mills' capabilities." He let the word 'special' linger with emphasis.

"This last time, Gustav showed up outside the bathroom. The first time I saw him was outside the Harrisons' bedroom. I need to find him again."

"That's interesting," Colter replied. "You guys can put this Lazarus anywhere a death occurred and it shows you what happened. But, Gustav didn't die up on the third floor."

"Are you sure about that?" Holbrook asked.

"Absolutely. He died in the dining room. The shooter came in through the servant's entrance by the pantry, passed through the kitchen, and shot Gustav while he was polishing silverware. There was an eyewitness. I am one hundred percent positive. The incident made the papers too."

"Perhaps," Holbrook mused, tapping his chin with a finger, "he's what we call an 'intelligent haunt.' Aware of his death and his surroundings. Unlike residuals, who are energy echoes, replaying their deaths over and over again, he seems to be capable of interaction. That makes him one of our best leads."

"Then we need to track him down," Coti said.

All eyes turned to Ryan, and they all had that same look. The *'Are you sure you want to do this again?'* look, and *'You're the only one that can do it.'*

Well, her head wasn't pounding, and no blood gushed from her nose this time. Maybe her body was getting used to the transition. But, she wasn't sure how used to it she wanted to get.

And if that thing she'd seen earlier wasn't Sam, then maybe she *could* face it again. That creature posing as someone didn't actually know anything about them. If that was true, she could do it again.

"Okay," she said, her fingers tightening into fists. "Let's do it."

"Where do we start?" Dave asked.

"Both times I saw Gustav, he was heading toward the stairs. Let's try the landing."

"All set to go, Ryan." Dave's fingers paused over the keyboard. The glow from the computer screen flared off his glasses as he looked at her over the top of the monitor.

Coti had set the Lazarus tripod at the top landing. From this position, it was a perfect view, albeit dark, down both corridors and the spiral staircase into the atrium. The familiar swarm of bees buzzed in her stomach, like they did moments before the tightness in her chest would start. She inhaled slowly, forcing the swarm into silence.

You can face it again. It's not him. It's not—and never will be—Sam.

Ryan sank down onto the carpet and crossed her legs, hands resting on her knees. "Ready when you are."

"Powering on." Dave clicked the *Enter* key. The cameras turned on, and Lazarus came to life, its blue laser grid sweeping over the room. Ryan closed her eyes as the hum climbed through her body like a tuning fork, synchronizing deep in her bones.

Visualize Gustav Liester—tuxedo, white towel over one arm—minus the hole in his head. The vibrations hummed deep into her core until they moved in sync throughout her body. The darkened staircase filled her mind, empty as it had been all night.

Then she felt the shift. She slowly opened her eyes to find the same emptiness, except sunlight poured in through the glass dome ceiling above, spilling down the gold chain of the chandelier, filling the staircase to the main floor atrium with warm light. The computers, the equipment, and the team were gone. Ryan sat alone at the top of the stairs.

She stood and checked both corridors. Nothing. She paced down the right-hand hallway and eased open the door to the third-floor bathroom. Light streamed through lace curtains onto a pristine, white room. Empty. No blood. No candle. No Gloria. She stepped back into the hall and scanned the length to the far end. No dark mist. No creature.

Her shoulders sank, and she called out to the empty floor. "Gustav? Mr. Liester?"

This wasn't the only floor in the mansion, but it was the only one where she had ever seen him. She had never strayed too far during her spirit walks, careful to remain within the device's locale. Now was as good a time as any to test the limits of Lazarus.

She moved back to the staircase and leaned over the railing. Nothing moved on either side of the second or third floor landings.

"Gustav?" she called again, louder this time. "Are you here? I need to talk to you."

Maybe no one dwelled in *this* portion of limbo. Still, Gloria Treadwell's Purgatory should not have overlapped with Gustav Liester's. He'd arrived long after the Treadwells had died, yet he still appeared in that moment—just as he had in the present.

Ryan descended the stairs, each step cushioned with a pristine plush carpet, to the main floor. Good so far. No weird side effects from straying away from Lazarus. The empty atrium glistened like something from a dream with the chandelier crystals scattering tiny rainbows throughout the room. *At least this Purgatory is beautiful.*

"Mr. Liester?"

"Do you intend to disturb the entire household with that racket?" the German-accented voice sounded behind her.

Gustav stood with his usual proper posture, white gloves and silver tray in one hand. He eyed her with a raised eyebrow.

"Gustav, I'm so glad I found you. I need your help."

"You have asked me, and I've already told you." He gazed down at her with one crooked eyebrow.

"Did you, though?" She let out an exasperated sigh. "I'm looking for a little girl. Emma. Have you seen her?"

He huffed, rolled his eyes, and started past her down the hall. "I have too much work to deal with your nonsense."

"Nonsense? She's missing. A little girl. I don't know if she is alive or—" Ryan hesitated. "Please, Gustav."

He sighed and turned, the light glinting off the silver tray. With rigid properness, he moved toward a long bench resting against the wall and sat, gesturing with a gloved hand to the space beside him. "Sit."

Maybe it was his accent or robot-like demeanor, but she sat beside him just as he demanded. No warmth exuded from his body, nor did she detect any scent. Perhaps in his day, he would have smelled like aftershave or wood polish.

He spoke first. "Answer me one question, will you?"

"Of course."

"Who are you? You come and go in brief flickers, and then I cannot find you again."

"You don't see us upstairs or . . . just when I see you?"

"Us?" His brow arched again. "There are more like you?"

She had to smile. It appeared that some of these specters don't realize that the living moved around them. "Yes. There are five of us in the house. I guess you can only see me."

"I sometimes glimpse people walking through here," he said, his gaze drifting to the crystals of the chandelier. "Like mirages—only for a few seconds and then they are gone. But only you linger."

She hesitated to say the next thought in her mind. "Do you know why you're still here?"

"Of course I do," he said with a scoff. "I manage the staff and this household. Without me, this place would descend into chaos."

"That's not what I meant."

"What you actually mean is, do I realize that I am dead." A half-grin formed on his lips. "I absolutely realize that. But I am still responsible for this house, and I will maintain it." He grew quiet, his gaze shifting to the windows, now dimming. "I've seen this girl you speak of many times. Glimpses here and there. Sometimes she sees me, too."

"She can see you?" Ryan's heart skipped.

He nodded. "Occasionally. But I have not seen her today, or maybe even yesterday, if I were to think about it."

"Would you be able to sense if she was . . . well, you know . . ."

"You mean dead, like me? Yes, I would. The aura would be

gone. That's how I know you walk where you do not belong. You have too many colors about you." He shot a furtive glance at the top of her head.

She wondered what those colors looked like and if they changed depending on her mood. In frantic times, it was probably dark blue. That was the color she could see when she was in pursuit of a suspect. Not completely blue, but just around the edges.

"What was her color?" she asked.

Gustav smiled, his gaze drifting to the window. "White, like a little angel."

In that moment, the room darkened as if a massive storm cloud had blocked out the sun. But this shadow was far darker than even a storm could create. Everything around them plunged into midnight, and all the lights in the house were as dark as they had been in her own world outside of Purgatory.

Gustav sucked in a breath, something that Ryan didn't realize a spirit could do. "It's looking for you. It knows you're here."

"The black mist?"

"The Beast," he said. "It feeds on pain. It's ancient, drawing spirits in like a magnet. I suspect it's why you're trapped."

Her eyes darted down the corridor, toward the wide-open doors of the dining hall. "What does it want?"

"Souls, of course. It is the very cause of so much despair in this house. It has been here as long as I have, and I've seen it do terrible things. We just call it The Beast. It has brought many lost spirits to this place because it needs to feed. And it always needs more. I suspect that is why you are trapped here."

"Did it kill the Harrisons?"

Deep furrows formed in his brow. "The Harrisons?"

"The family who died on the third floor? The girl I'm looking for?"

He closed his eyes, and then the lines smoothed. "Ah, yes. Master Harrison. I do suspect the family will be expecting dinner soon." The butler leaned a hand on the arm of the chair and moved to get up, but Ryan stopped him.

"Gustav. Wait. I need to know what happened here."

Heavy footsteps thundered along the second-floor hallway above their heads, racing from one end of the house to the other. Goosebumps raised on Ryan's forearms as both she and Gustav looked to the ceiling.

"You must leave this place," he said, his voice dropping to a whisper. "You cannot allow it to find you here." He glanced over her shoulder and down the hall. "And take your little friend with you. He does not belong in the house. He knows that. Gets the floors soaking wet and creates more work for me."

Ryan shot a look behind her, but there was nothing but hallways cloaked in darkness. "Who are you talking about? I didn't bring anyone."

"Oh, yes you did," he said, standing, setting his jaw until his lips were a thin line. "He's been following you since you arrived. But he knows the rules. He's not allowed inside the house. Now go. Both of you."

She again glanced back down the hallway. Nobody from the team had followed her. That would have been impossible for her not to notice. And that could only mean one other thing.

"Gustav," she said, forcing her voice to remain steady, "this one who follows me, is he dead?"

"I do not see an aura, so what do you think?"

The pounding footsteps raced back across the second floor. The ground trembled with each step, an urgency that Ryan could no longer ignore. That thing was desperate to find her.

"Go, now!" Gustav shouted and then ran down the corridor.

He glanced back once before ducking into the dining hall and slamming the doors behind him.

The stomping sounded on the staircase. Then another sound followed it, like an insect clicking and hissing its way along the walls. Ryan closed her eyes and held her breath.

Get me out of here now. Take me back to Lazarus. Now.

The footsteps became a sprint as a cold rush of putrid wind blasted her back. Cold. Furious.

Get me out of here, Lazarus. Take me back! Ryan screamed in her mind—

—and then she vanished.

CHAPTER 19

Blue lights pulsed beyond her closed eyelids, outside the realm of Purgatory. Heavy footfalls sprinted down the hallway toward her, and the beast breathed out a screeching howl.

And then it was gone.

Hands grabbed her as she swayed backward. "I'm here," Matt whispered, catching her in his arms.

The darkness of the third-floor landing surrounded her, along with the four others who had witnessed the events through Lazarus—everything except her conversation with Gustav. If Lazarus could record audio, then Gustav's message would offer some clarity to the images they'd witnessed.

Her spine remained rigid as a throbbing pain bloomed at the base of her skull, worming its way behind her eyes. Holbrook lifted her under her arms, helping her to stand. The effort sent the room spinning.

"Here." Coti offered her a tissue. "For your nose."

With a trembling hand, Ryan wiped the trickle of moisture under her nose, leaving a dark crimson stain on the tissue. Pain bore into her forehead, creating a pattern of sparking lights in the darkness. She took a step, but her legs buckled, and Holbrook caught her again.

"Alright," he said, steering her toward the chaise against the far wall overlooking the landing. "Rest here."

She collapsed onto the lounger and closed her eyes. The flashing lights faded, but the headache persisted, pulsing with every heartbeat.

"I don't think Emma is in the house," she said softly. "Gustav hasn't seen her since it happened."

Holbrook lifted her legs onto the chair and nudged her into a recline across the plush surface. She didn't object, mainly because it would require opening her eyes.

"No more of this tonight," he said, sitting beside her. "We wait until dawn. The other agents are bound to come looking for us if we don't check in."

"If she's still alive, she might not be by dawn." Ryan's voice caught. She had to hope that Emma had somehow survived the massacre of her family. That she had had the wits to run from the house and hide, even though an entire FBI team and the local sheriff's department had found no sign of her on the estate grounds.

"We've done all we can," he said.

"No." Ryan forced her eyes open and sat up. "I can still do this. Matt, I *need* to do this—for Emma."

His hand pressed gently on her shoulder, easing her back against the cushions. "I will not allow any more of this."

Her eyebrow rose, despite the stab of pain it triggered. "You won't allow? Excuse me, but I'm a Special Agent with the FBI."

A coy grin crept over his lips. "Are you now?"

"And I have a gun."

"Oh, I see. And are you prepared to shoot me, then?"

"If it comes to that," she said, managing a smile. "But I'm serious about continuing. I'm getting close. I can feel it."

His shoulders slumped. In the darkness, his broad brow line left shadows over the dark brown eyes that looked at her.

"Ryan, we don't know the long-term effects of repeated exposure to the EMF."

"I understand that, but I'm willing to take that chance."

"But what if I am not?" He stared into the vast emptiness of the hallway.

Holbrook exhaled, the weight of the moment pressing into silence. The light caught the strands of his hair, lessening his appearance as a scientist and more as the man behind the role.

"There's something else," she whispered. "I think someone is following me in there."

"What do you mean?"

"Gustav said there was someone with me, someone who had died. A *he*. What if it's Sam? What if he *is* still trying to . . . haunt me?"

"Have you seen him, other than what the demon mimicked?"

She hesitated. "I'm not sure. But I feel it—someone watching me when I'm alone. In my house. At the lab. Even here."

He went still. "If it's truly him, there may not be much we can do, I'm afraid."

Ryan winced as the pain pulsed behind her eyes.

Holbrook placed his hand on hers. "At least give me this: we take a break. Let yourself recover before doing another spirit walk. Deal?"

She nodded, the motion making her dizzy. "Deal."

Holbrook gave her leg a gentle pat and stood, crossing to the computer table where Dave finished shutting down the Lazarus system.

"Everyone will take a break. It's extremely late and we are all exhausted."

"What time is it?" Coti asked.

Colter pulled back the sleeve of his jacket and glanced at his watch. "Little after one."

"And I checked again," Dave said. "Still no cell signal."

"Yeah, and none of the windows will budge," Coti muttered.

"We keep checking." Holbrook stuffed his hands into his pants pockets. "But for now, we're stuck here. I suggest getting some rest, for an hour at least."

Coti nodded. "No objection here."

Holbrook returned to the chaise and sat on the floor against the side of the seat.

"You don't have to keep an eye on me," Ryan said. The faint scent of Matt's shampoo drifted toward her.

"I know. But what if I get lonely?"

She gave a small laugh.

"Or scared?" he said.

"Then I probably won't be much help."

He leaned his head back against the cushion. Ryan's hand found his hair, and her fingers lightly massaged his head.

"Not much of a friend in need," he murmured, "but you are a good masseuse."

"I do have my good points."

"No more talking," he said, though he made no move to stop her hand. "You need to rest for a while."

"Wake me up in an hour if I fall asleep."

He nodded as her fingers continued to move through his hair.

CHAPTER 20

Dave woke with a start from where he rested on his crossed arms upon the computer table. Not the most comfortable position, but enough to get a little rest. Down the hall, the sheriff's faint snores cut through the quiet, and Coti shifted from where she lay on one of the four chaise loungers across from him. A dull ache pulsed between his shoulders as he pushed himself upright and adjusted his crooked glasses.

It couldn't have been more than thirty minutes since they agreed to take a break, but it felt like hours. The monitor screensaver bounced colorful ribbons across the black screen. Red and blue light reflected off his glasses, highlighting dust spots that had accumulated throughout the day.

He leaned back against the soft vinyl of his wheelchair, stretching until his spine gave a satisfying pop along the vertebrae in his thoracic spine. Light from the monitor glowed against his wristwatch: 2:27 a.m. Still no cell service. His wife had expected a check-in call at least two hours ago, 10 p.m. her time, about when she put their two girls to bed. Whenever he was out on assignment, he always called to wish them goodnight. Amy was going to worry, but there was nothing he could do.

A thud echoed from down the far end of the hallway.

Dave froze, and his breath caught as he peered over the top of the monitor and into the gloom of the corridor. Only the occasional shafts of moonlight fell through the windows in illuminated patches, leaving the gaps between in darkness.

Maybe it's the house settling. That's normal, right? Old places shifted and shuddered in the dark. But this house wasn't normal, and that made the hair rise on the back of his neck. This place thrived within some dimension where only Ryan could actually see or hear. So it had to be the house, right?

Another thud. Louder. Closer.

He snapped the laptop closed and stared down the corridor. Silence returned except for the occasional whisper of the breeze against the windowpanes.

He glanced at Coti, her head resting on her wadded-up sweatshirt. Neither she nor the others stirred. Two thuds from a supposedly empty house weren't enough to wake them.

The wheels were cold in his hands as he rolled back from the table. Too many wild thoughts swam in his head. A smirk tugged at the edge of his goatee. If he woke Ryan over a possible raccoon rattling a window, she'd never let him live it down. And neither would Coti. She'd never stop teasing. And Doc? He'd drone on for days about data contamination from ambient noise.

No. He'd check out the scene—quietly. If it was nothing, okay, but if it was Emma . . .

The thought of Emma Harrison made his stomach twist—bright-eyed, smiling. What if that sound was her trying to make herself known, scared and alone, now that the mansion was finally quiet?

The chair rolled in near silence along the antique rug stretched throughout the third-floor landing. Dave scanned the corridor ahead for any sign of movement, either in the shafts of light or within the shadows between. As he approached the first room, his stomach turned and left a thick spasm in his throat. The middle boy's room still bore the mark of his murder across the sheets and walls. He didn't want to look, and despite his disbelief in superstition, he definitely didn't want to go in that room alone. The door still stood ajar. Yet, in the absence of power, the room had now plunged into a deep black where even moonlight from the hallway couldn't penetrate.

He rolled past the open doorway and toward the next, which offered little comfort—just as dark, just as dead. As the coppery stench of old blood hung in the air, he moved into the space between them.

The third room was Emma's, and, thankfully, was devoid of the horrors staining the other two. He paused, breath slowing, pulse steadying. It's nothing. *Only the house settling.* Exactly as he had suspected.

He started to pivot when a flash of white darted across his vision. In that second, he could have sworn a child ran from a shaft of moonlight into the dark and then plunged into the girl's room. Or maybe it was a trick of the light in a tremendously creepy house that held them captive, along with whatever lurked in the halls and the barn.

Dave swallowed. "Hello?" he whispered.

His fingers curled into white knuckles around the wheels. *No*, he thought. *Only Ryan can see this stuff, right?*

He glanced behind him again. Everyone lay exactly how they had been. Still sleeping. Still unaware.

A child's giggle echoed from Emma's room. His head whipped back to the darkened room. That was real. He hadn't imagined it.

His heart jackhammered in his chest. The wheelchair suddenly felt like it weighed heavier than possible. He could barely push his arms along the wheels. Then a blur shifted in the room ahead.

"Emma?" he breathed. He sucked in a breath and held it again as he listened to every sound that came from the corridor or the room. Five, ten seconds ticked by. Nothing. The breath slipped from his throat, and his fingers relaxed on the wheels.

"Is that you, Emma? We're here to help you."

Another giggle, but this time, there was another voice behind it. A growl tangled within the child's laugh, twisting into a noise neither human nor animal.

Dave recoiled.

That was *no* little girl.

A gust of icy, dank air crept from the room, thick with rot and memory. Like a meat locker. A place full of dripping blood and death. Then a sound that rippled over his skin and sank into his spine.

David—

What the…

David froze when, beyond the door, within the darkness, something slithered. Blackness against black. It felt serpentine, with smoke curling from its open mouth, ready to devour him. This thing exuded fear and hatred. Exactly how Ryan had described it.

Dave gripped the wheels tighter and rolled them backward. A shadow crept around the edge of the doorway, its tendrils pooling onto the hallway carpet like ink spilling into clear water, casting even the moonlight in shadow as it advanced. He rolled back further, his fingers grabbing the wheels in desperation.

David—

It knew his name. Probably knew everything about him. Ryan had been right: an evil had infected this house.

The dark wisps stretched into vines across the hallway floor, stretching and curling toward him. He gripped further down the front of the wheels, pulling hard, while keeping his eyes trained on the thing in front of him. Afraid it would lunge if he turned.

I know you, David—

"Hey." Coti's voice snapped through the air.

He jumped, and the chair jerked to a stop as it bumped into something behind him. His head swiveled back to see her face looking down at him. Her hand rested on his shoulder. "What's up? You're shaking."

The icy grip he had on the wheels loosened, and he spun a glance back toward the gaping door of Emma's room. It stood empty. Still. No shadowy tentacles inching toward him. No monstrous laughter.

"I saw—" The words caught in his throat like plaster. If he described what happened, it would sound unbelievable. Maybe he was tired. They *had* been there for hours.

"You saw something?" Coti leaned down to peer along his line of sight.

He shook his head. "I don't know. Probably shadows. Tricks of the light."

"In this place?" Her voice dipped. "I wouldn't be too sure of that."

"Yeah. I think it's just getting to me."

"Come on." She grasped the wheelchair handles and turned the chair gently. "You need rest as much as the rest of us. And we need to stick together. This place is way too creepy to be going off on your own."

He forced a grin. "Okay, mom."

Coti rolled the chair up to the table and, after locking the wheels, she settled next to him. Nobody else had heard their whispers and still remained asleep. Dave rested against the back, his spine finally loosening enough to feel his shoulders relax.

"The sun can't come up soon enough," he whispered.

A slow breath filled Coti's lungs. "I know. I hate this place."

The empty hallway stared at him with a soulless gaze. Although he knew that nothing was there, the hair on his neck still stood on end. He gave one last look toward Emma's door.

"What do you think is back there?" Coti asked, her hand moved to his forearm.

A shudder moved along his spine. "I don't think that little girl is alive. I think we're looking for a corpse."

"Why? What's going on?"

"Whatever this thing is, it's playing with us."

"Did you see it back there, in her room?" Coti's voice dropped.

The darkness beyond the door remained still, but it seemed so much blacker now. Deeper. Hungry. The shuddering moved from his bones and into his core, leaving a chill that pushed into the sinew of his arms. Whatever was in this place, it was ancient, cruel. The things that he had experienced were only for him to see. He couldn't explain what he saw, not in a way she'd believe. But he believed Ryan now. All of it.

Something evil and inhuman dwelt within this place. It had tried to lure him away from the light. That little girl couldn't survive something like that. David was sure of it. All they could do now was last until morning. Live through the night until someone—anyone—came to get them the hell out of here.

CHAPTER 21

It lies to them.

Ryan's eyes snapped open, and she bolted upright at the whisper fading in her ear. The breath of it lingered against her skin, but the voice had already gone. Down the corridor, Coti stood beside Dave, both staring into the darkness of the opposite hallway in silence as if expecting something to happen. They were too far away to have whispered anything to her.

Matt snored from where he leaned against the chaise in front of her, every breath slow and steady. It couldn't have been him either.

She swung her legs around until her feet met the ground. Everything in the hallway had grown darker than when she'd closed her eyes, the sounds sharper, the silence too crisp. But no further whispers.

She examined the shadows in the hallway, every corner around her.

"Everything okay?" Coti whispered.

"I thought I heard something," Ryan murmured.

The sound of breaking glass from somewhere in the mansion startled everyone. Matt jumped awake. Colter scrambled upright with a hand on his holster. "What the hell was that?" he exclaimed.

Coti ran to the banister and peered down to the lower floors. "I think it came from the first floor."

Ryan appeared at her side, heart pounding. The first-floor entrances had been impenetrable, and that likely hadn't changed in the last couple of hours. She withdrew her flashlight from her belt and aimed it down the spiral banister toward the darkness three floors below—the circle of light barely reaching the antique carpet of the first-floor landing.

"Do you see anything?" Holbrook's voice startled her. He was so close to her ear, she flinched and almost dropped the flashlight.

Ryan shook her head as she gazed down the length of the beam.

"I'll go check it out," Colter said as he stepped up to the banister.

Ryan nodded and reached for her sidearm. "I'm going with you."

"Mind if I tag along?" Holbrook asked.

"Just stay behind me, Doc."

She gave the *go-ahead* nod to Watson, and they proceeded down the stairway, shoulder to shoulder, guns drawn. Ryan trained on the dark landing where it opened into the grand atrium. No signs of broken glass. No evidence of an intruder.

Colter broke left as Ryan turned right, flanking toward the front doors. She tested the knob. It didn't budge. They were still locked in the mansion.

"Front door clear," she called.

"West hall clear," Colter responded.

Ryan glanced up the stairway where Matt waited. She nodded, and he descended the last few steps into the atrium as she lowered her weapon. When Colter joined them, all eyes turned toward the darkness of the east corridor.

"I don't get it," she said. "It sounded like a window shattered, but there's nothing. No glass."

"I'll go check out the kitchen and dining hall." Colter ticked his head back down the west corridor.

Ryan nodded, flicking the beam back down the east corridor where the void devoured the light before it reached the end of the hall. "Doc and I will check out the conservatory and the pools." She turned back to Matt, whose eyes had grown wide enough for the whites to be apparent, even in the dim atrium.

"You think you'll be alright by yourself, Colter?"

The sheriff let out a nervous laugh. "I never liked walking these halls on my own even when I did know what was lurking around the corners. But, yeah, I'll be okay."

They split up. Matt shuffled close enough behind her that she could feel his body heat as they inched down the corridor. Ryan held the flashlight and pistol along the same trajectory as her gaze darted to every corner, beyond each door. Somewhere along this seemingly endless passage lay the entrances to the globe-like conservatory. She remembered it from the tour—an architectural marvel made entirely of leaded glass. It would be the most logical place for someone to break into the house. But it was located so far from the mansion's core, and the sound of broken glass had emanated nearer to the atrium. Not out here.

And then there was the obvious: the house was sealed. Locked tight by some supernatural force. There was no way the conservatory had suddenly become accessible.

The same fact applied to the pools. Massive decks of sliding glass doors—each sealed by the unseen force that had kept them imprisoned. Yet, the closer she and Matt came to the end of the corridor, the heavier the scent of chlorine hung in the air.

A second, smaller hallway split from the main hall, merging with a short tunnel on the right. Ryan turned her light toward the set of glass doors with a security pad on the door handle.

Stepping closer, she gazed through the glass into the stillness. Tranquil swimming pools glimmered under moonlight, their surfaces undisturbed. Ripples of light shimmered across the water and spilled into the hallway, dancing gently across tile and glass.

Ryan tested the door. The handle didn't budge.

"I could try to smash the glass, but I'm pretty sure I know what would happen," Matt whispered.

"A whole lot of nothing," she responded. No broken glass or prowlers walked around the pools. And no shadowed tentacles slithered from the corners of the room.

"I don't get it, Doc. We definitely heard something."

Matt moved closer, his eyes remaining fixed on the peaceful, moonlit scene. "Perhaps something is trying to get our attention."

Ryan had the same feeling—that they were not only prisoners but being toyed with. That something was ramping up the tension and gorging itself on the emotional results.

They wandered back into the main hall, and she turned the flashlight toward the corridor's terminus. *Finally, the end of the west corridor.* Turning, they headed back toward the conservatory.

"The big question is: what is trying to get our attention?" Holbrook gently grasped her arm, and she turned to face him. "Is it the elemental or is it the spirits that haunt this place?"

"And why now? Why would either of them want our attention at this very moment?"

His smile did not offer comfort. It was the kind that made her skin crawl—the kind you see moments before the monster crawls out of the sewer to grab some kids and pull them into the dark to devour them. Anytime something wanted attention in a horror movie, it was always a diversion.

There was no broken glass. Only a phantom sound, like so many in this house. And there would be more.

Ryan nodded. "You're right." Her eyes wandered past him to the end of the corridor, to the massive iron-and-glass doors that barred the entry to the conservatory. The flashlight's beam glinted off the panes as she stepped closer and focused on the conservatory dome.

"I've got another burning question, Doc. I can't believe I just now thought of this."

"Ask away."

"That thing—whatever it is—can't seem to find me like it did in the stables. Why? When I spirit walk, it hunts me. It *senses* me when I'm there. But inside the house? It's like it can't track me. And it hasn't hurt any of you either. At least not yet. Its powers must work differently in here than they do outside."

"Hmm," Matt murmured, leaning closer to the glass. "You're right. It hasn't touched us. You said it dragged you across the ground, yet in here you are unscathed, as are the rest of us. I have no explanation for that."

Ryan gripped the iron handle of the door. Still locked. Nothing had changed. Moonlight fell in soft, silver waves across the plants, casting deep green shadows that arced over patches of black space that sank deep into the large room.

Turning back toward the hallway, Ryan raised the flashlight—and caught sudden movement. Her other hand instinctively twitched toward her sidearm. Then Colter raised an arm to shield his eyes from the beam.

"Man, I could have shot you," she said, her fingers slipping away from her firearm and the light drifting back toward the ground. "You're too quiet."

"I've got nothing on my end of the building," he said. "You guys find anything?"

She shook her head. "Nothing."

Matt hadn't noticed Ryan step away from the conservatory door. His hand still rested against the glass as he peered into the darkest recesses of the room, where large palm leaves dipped over into the moonlight filtering through the glass panels overhead. His eyes followed that light as it cascaded in waves of silver over plants, sinking into dark shadows, until he saw her.

A woman. No more than twenty, thin and beautiful, but a creature out of place, like a faded photograph of another era. Short flaxen hair swept around her angled, smooth face, with lips painted in the same red lacquer and cupid bow as seen on vintage starlets of the silent film era. But her pale, gray skin held the lifeless tone of someone long dead. And her eyes were clouded over like an old milk glass.

She stood like a statue and watched him.

Any other night, Holbrook would've chalked it up to exhaustion or a figment of his imagination. But not here. Not now. Not in a mansion that refused to let them leave. He wanted to look away, to call out for Ryan, but the woman's eyes had lured him in. And in that hollow gaze, thoughts poured into his mind. Whispered fragments. Unwanted secrets from the shadows, where she had to remain.

Her lips curved into a wide grin, but they didn't move. Yet the whispers continued to press into Holbrook's mind. Secrets that only he should know.

And though you walk through the valley of the shadow of death, you should fear this evil.

CHAPTER 22

"Everything okay?" Ryan said, grasping Matt's shoulder.

He jumped and turned to face her. The color had drained from his face, and his eyes were wide.

"What's going on, Doc?"

He glanced back through the conservatory windows. "I-I thought I saw something."

Colter approached and peered in. "Someone's in there?"

"That's not possible," Ryan said, stepping closer.

They stood in silence, eyes fixed on the room's inky shadows. Nothing but the quiet stillness of plants soaking in the night. Ryan's breath fogged against the glass as she scanned every inch of the space. Not a soul could have gotten into this house without them knowing it. If something had been in there, she would have seen it.

"I don't see anyone," Colter said.

Matt rubbed at his eyes with trembling hands. "I-I must be tired." Colter gave the man's shoulder a light squeeze and guided him away, but Ryan lingered. This mansion held its secrets within its shadows, and she didn't trust it at all.

"I think we're all a little tired and rattled, Doc," Colter said. "Let's get out of here."

Ryan's voice dropped as she continued peering into the dark room. "What did you see, Matt?"

"It was nothing."

"You know we don't believe in *nothing*." Her tone carried a slight edge.

"Really, Ryan. I think I'm just tired."

She stood straighter and turned to face him. "Okay. I understand." The flashlight weighed heavier in her tight grip. "Colter, take Doc back upstairs. I'll be right behind you. I want to check all the windows around the conservatory."

Both men gave her a concerned look.

Ryan sighed. "I promise, I'll be okay. I'll be up in a few minutes."

Colter clicked his tongue. "Fine. But I'm only giving you five minutes before I send in a search party."

"Copy that." She smiled and turned back to the door, watching Colter and Matt's reflections in the glass until they disappeared down the hallway.

Her reflection stared back from the black panes. She didn't want to be alone, but she *had* to get Holbrook away from the conservatory. Everything in her gut told her that something was wrong with this room. It had affected him, whether he admitted it or not. The flashlight was her only lifeline, and it was barely enough.

There was little sound beyond her own breathing or the whistling breeze outside. She tapped her fingernail against the glass. A footstep echoed a response along the stone floor inside.

She held her breath. That wasn't her fingernail. It was deliberate. A hard-soled shoe, very close. Raising the flashlight, Ryan swept the beam wildly across the conservatory, angling for the deeper shadows. Back and forth until she stopped, letting the beam settle to her feet. She couldn't look at it with tense and panicked eyes.

Just breathe. Ryan closed her eyes and inhaled slowly. Letting her breath out slowly, she let her shoulders fall, releasing the tension. The weight of the flashlight lightened, and she clicked it off, allowing the natural moonlight of the night to filter through the glass.

Ryan stood taller and faced the door, the vision clearer now. She could see what had occurred in that space so long ago . . .

The humid air thickened, fragrant with the sweetness of orchids and gardenia. Strands of tiny incandescent bulbs floated along electrical wires like fireflies among the foliage. A phonograph played a scratchy big-band tune—brass horns lifting through the leaves. Laughter, clinking glasses. A party in full swing.

A couple drifted past her, hand-in-hand, stepping through the glass door as if it weren't there. They laughed, inebriated with celebration, and joined the crowd of guests who had been in the room the entire time. Red, white, and blue bunting surrounded the scene—it was a century-old Independence Day celebration.

As the song faded, the lights dimmed, and the laughter vanished into silence, as did the guests. The palms no longer shimmered with light. All was shadow, again.

Except for one figure that stared at her from under a tree.

Ryan squinted, then flicked the flashlight on. A blonde woman, thin and frail. This was not her imagination. The woman tilted her chin down, and her lips curled into a slow, knowing grin that bared sharp, glassy teeth dripping with venom. A grotesque contrast to her once beautiful face.

This was no harmless spirit of the house vying for her attention. This was the dark entity that had taken hold of Chad Harrison and now had found a way to manifest itself into a lie. It had probably worn this form before to others that had crossed its path. Maybe it fooled Emma, too. But Ryan knew it for what it was.

She stepped away from the glass panes and let the light fall away from the creature's face. There was no telling what this thing would do if she stared at it any longer, and she didn't want to find out.

As Ryan headed away from the conservatory, an ethereal voice filled her mind:

I'll see you soon.

CHAPTER 23

Coti's fingers clutched the banister as she watched over half of the team descend the spiral staircase with weapons drawn. That left her alone with Dave. And while she really loved the guy, he was already acting strange and seeing things down the hall. That, plus they stood on the same floor where four people had been murdered only a couple of days ago. It was enough to put anyone on edge.

Ryan and the others disappeared on the first floor, chasing the source of the disturbance, leaving Coti and Dave to monitor the third floor with the equipment. As she watched the others fade into the atrium's darkness, it was only then that she realized how hard she'd been gripping the banister.

"I bet they won't find anything," Dave whispered from behind her.

She turned, goosebumps rising along her back. "I really hope they don't."

"It's this place. It's messing with us."

That was the *last* thing she needed to hear—that a building could physically *manipulate* people. It was one thing for Ryan to see and hear these things, but it was an entirely different problem if the unseen could interact with the rest of them. Coti didn't want any part of it. She just wanted to do her job—record the images Lazarus provided, work through the problem, and move on.

She hugged her arms tightly around her torso, trying to abate the shivers that lingered across her skin. This place never seemed to warm up since the power went out. The cold seeped into her bones, and it would probably only get colder until the sun rose.

"Sorry," Dave muttered. "I think I left my jacket in the van."

"It's okay. It probably wouldn't help anyway. It's this place."

"I know, right. Like it'll never be warm again." He turned to face her when a *whir* sound cut through the silence, making Coti and Dave snap their heads toward the table.

"Was that you?" she whispered.

Dave shook his head.

The video cameras, still mounted on their tripods around the mini-Lazarus, independently rotated inward. One by one, they pointed toward the center—as if awaiting activation. Coti slipped close to Dave, her throat tight as the monitor flickered out of sleep mode. Something had powered it up.

"What's happening?" she said.

Dave opened his laptop, entered his passcode, and stared at the display. His shaking hands hovered over the keyboard, but he didn't speak.

"Dave?"

"I-I don't know. Something started Lazarus."

"Some*thing*?"

The mini-Lazarus powered up. Blue light pulsed inside the device, casting a laser grid cascade across the third-floor landing.

Coti stepped back, her heart hammering against her ribs. Her mind raced, searching behind the table, through the shadows around him, and in the equipment cases. *Where are they?* She crouched, her fingers opening one of the hard cases under the table until she found them. The spectacles. Grabbing two pairs, she placed one on her face and handed another to Dave just as the laser grid flashed over the area around them.

The cameras started recording on their own. Coti rose to her feet, glancing between the grid and monitor. Whatever happened now, she had to watch. This wasn't a planned recording, and she had no idea how it happened.

Through the lenses, the landing glowed a pale blue. Everything—the banister, the stairs, the carpet—was awash in its pale glow. And the cameras continued recording, panning the room as if expecting someone to appear.

Every beat of her heart thudded in Coti's ears.

"Doc needs to know about this," Dave said.

"About what? Do you see *anything* yet?" she whispered.

"Nothing." Dave said, fingers racing over the keyboard. The monitor to his right displayed current EMF readings as flat over a steady and continuous line. "I don't know what's going on."

The steady line flickered, causing a sudden spike in the green line. The blue light cast over the landing faltered, then something appeared within the left edge of the Lazarus perimeter. At first, Coti thought it was only drifting dust, but it moved too fast.

"What is that?" Coti breathed as a figure formed in the light. First, a leg, then the shape of a torso.

"Is that . . . ?" Dave gasped.

Gloria Treadwell. Alive. Healthy. Nothing like the last time with her wrists cut in the bathtub. She stepped across the landing, her sequined dress glistening around her body, and disappeared as she moved through the blue light and onto the stairs. A shadow of the past, walking, as she once had, through *her* house.

Another person entered the light—an unknown man in a sharp suit, clearly from the same era as Gloria's. Neither acknowledged Coti's nor Dave's presence. They drifted through the Lazarus light like echoes.

Then came a woman wearing a black dress with a white apron and her hair pinned back. The maid's attire appeared older, from decades earlier than the Treadwells. She paused, dusted her apron, then turned as though someone had called her name. A second maid stepped into view, carrying a silver tray. They exchanged silent words, then descended the stairs together.

"What are we seeing? It's like watching a silent movie only . . . it isn't," Coti said.

Dave shook his head. "It's a recording of decades of activity in this house. Not sure why we're seeing it, though. It's not trauma. It's just . . . life."

After the maids had stepped out of view, the scene remained vacant. Coti's breathing steadied, as did the EMF readings on the monitor. No further spikes along the baseline.

The house wanted to show them something, but why? It was so mundane. Everyday life on the third-floor landing. Nothing special, but for some reason, the house, or something, took over the cameras so Lazarus could show them people from its past.

Coti hugged her arms close, allowing the goosebumps to subside, while watching the perimeter for any other signs of activity.

Another flash of light played at the edges, shimmering as if something tried to enter the Lazarus display. It flickered for several moments, then someone burst into the scene.

A girl danced across the landing, hair in a ponytail, tights, and a spring dress.

"That's her, Emma Harrison," Coti breathed.

Emma danced around the landing, her fingers trailing along the banister posts, her joyful smile shining in the blue laser light.

She stopped at the top of the stairs and looked at something at the far end of the hall, out of view from the Lazarus display. Her mouth moved in words they couldn't hear as she spoke to someone taller than herself.

The figure entered the scene, and Coti felt all breath suck from her lungs. Her hand flew to her mouth as she stepped back, pressing against the wall behind her.

"No. No. No. No," she whimpered.

"That's not possible," Dave gasped, his fingers tapping on the keyboard, zooming in on the monitor.

The man entered the scene and reached out toward the little girl.

"No!" Coti yelled. "Leave her alone!" Her fingers clutched into a fist as she watched.

Emma didn't recoil. She stood there as the man stepped closer. Then he lunged, hands wrapping about the little girl's throat. She struggled, her tiny legs kicking until he tossed her small body over the railing.

Dave and Coti gasped, frozen.

The man lingered a moment, watching Emma fall over the edge, then turned toward them, his face clear within the square of the Lazarus device.

They knew that face.

Sam.

Their former supervisor. Special agent of the FBI. A serial killer. A man who was dead.

Dave typed furiously. The laser light made every feature sickeningly clear. No matter the angle, it was him, down to the cold stare he had the last moment Coti had seen him. And worse, Sam *saw* them. His eyes tracked their movement, following Coti as she shifted.

This was no recording.

"Shut it down, Dave." She slipped behind Dave's chair. "Shut it down, now!"

"I'm trying." The EMF readings spiked like jagged teeth. Coti's fingernails pressed into the wheelchair cushions, her eyes wide as Sam watched her.

"Got it!" They watched the EMF line go flat before the monitor blinked off.

"He's still there, Dave."

"That's impossible." Dave's fingers flew across the keyboard, but the laser grid remained active, and the cameras kept recording.

"Turn it off, please," she whimpered.

"I'm trying! The system isn't responding."

She glanced at the monitor as Dave worked. The cameras recorded every angle displayed on the screen. The laser representation of Sam continued to watch her from the Lazarus perimeter, still and quiet. If she removed her glasses, she knew he'd still be there even if she couldn't see him.

Sam's grin widened, a grotesque twist on an already-unsettling, dead face. Coti trembled uncontrollably, and each breath from her lips sent white puffs into the air as the temperature dropped around them.

"You've got to turn it off," she pleaded.

"I can't. It's not working." Dave glanced up at Coti. "I-I'm sorry."

Suddenly, Sam moved, bursting into a sprint, his body arcing toward them. In an instant, he'd crossed the length of the Lazarus square, past the grid line, and lunged toward the monitor table.

Coti jumped back, braced for impact, but nothing happened. The image vanished, leaving the perimeter empty.

Coti pulled the glasses from her face. At that moment, the folding chair next to her flew across the floor and crashed into the banister. The air around them chilled further. A cold breeze pierced the air, causing the hallway curtains to shift. Shadows twisted and curled in on themselves.

"Watch out!" Dave grabbed Coti's wrist, pulling her to the right seconds before the chaise next to her overturned and was thrown against the opposite wall.

Then everything went silent.

The air warmed. The grid flickered out. The cameras stopped recording, and the program shut down.

Dave's voice was barely a whisper. "I don't think that was Sam."

CHAPTER 24

Ryan pushed away from the conservatory's glass doors, an effort that was more difficult than she'd expected. Colter and Doc had left, but she was never truly *alone*. Now, Gustav's comment came to her mind, and the thought of something following her, unseen in the dark, made her blood run cold.

She willed the flashlight to shine brighter, but shadows appeared to consume every ounce of light. Her footsteps echoed off the walls, overlapping with the next, until the rising sound closed in, as if something was just inches behind her.

Ryan slowed to a stop—and so did *it*.

Someone followed me here.

Was it possible? Could *he* have that much power in the afterlife?

No. I won't believe it. I can't.

Perhaps it was someone else. Yes, it had to be. Gustav hadn't been afraid of the intruder—more annoyed, really.

"Hello? Is someone there?"

She waited, listening. Sweat formed on her brow as the beam strained to pierce the darkness. Whatever was out there lingered beyond its reach. The corridor appeared empty, just as she'd expected, but she knew it was far from it. Nothing walked behind her, at least nothing she could see. Ryan rubbed the back of her neck. Maybe she couldn't see it, but she felt it. Somewhere.

A Man Who Wasn't There.

The light beam wavered in her trembling hand. Cold-blooded killers, instinct-driven murderers—*those* she could handle. But the unseen—the unknown entities she and Holbrook had just begun to investigate—*they* made her uneasy. There was no defense against them. Silently, they could slither close and touch her. Or worse—do things she didn't yet understand.

Ryan swept the flashlight from side to side and continued down the corridor. The spiral staircase's landing was in front of her. Behind, the stalker's footsteps resumed—faster now.

"Hello?" she said again, slowing her pace once more. She glanced at her watch, dark and silent. Whatever it was, it didn't want to reveal itself—not even to mini-Lazarus.

Then came another footstep. Then another. And another. Soft. Measured. Pacing—but keeping its distance.

It wasn't stalking her.

It was *hunting* her.

Panic seized every muscle in her body. Her lifeline—the staircase, the team, Matt—lay just ahead. If she could reach them, she wouldn't be alone, even if The Man was right behind her.

She bolted, boots pounding against the floor. Her pursuer launched into a run—faster, closing in. The beam spun wildly with each stride, strobing across the corridor walls. The staircase appeared, and she leapt for it. Landing on the third step, she bounded upward.

Three steps. Six. Nine.

Above, she heard the faint chatter of her team. She tried to yell, but terror held her voice captive. *I am here. I am here.* Her heart pounded, threatening to explode.

Can't stop. Almost there. Almost . . .

Her lungs burned and her limbs felt heavy, like wading through water. It was getting closer. She could smell . . . death.

Something growled behind her—hot, guttural, snapping at her heels. She grabbed the banister, pulling herself faster. The second-floor landing opened, and Ryan swung around the curve, sprinting toward the final flight.

The creature's breath blistered the backs of her legs. She wanted to scream for help, but didn't dare waste what strength she had left. The staircase curved to the left; only a dozen or more steps to go. When the landing came into view, she could see mini-Lazarus, the cameras, and the monitor table. Even Doc and Colter had made it back.

She leaped for the last few stairs and tumbled onto the landing, rolling onto her back, her flashlight clattering to the floor as she instinctively trained her weapon on whatever might follow. She inhaled deeply, chest heaving, eyes fixed on the dark stairwell, the tension pressing like a vice, seconds ticking by as she waited for the attack.

No creature snarled. No phantom pounced. Whatever had chased her was gone.

"Everything okay?" Colter asked.

Her flashlight lay by his feet, its beam lifeless. The darkness beyond the edge of the stairs remained that—a shadowy silence in an endless void.

Yet, it was still out there, waiting. For her.

Slowly, she moved farther away from the stairs. She looked up at Coti's wide eyes and pale face. Dave's worried expression behind his glasses. None of them was okay.

Ryan rested on the chaise, sipping from the water bottle Holbrook had offered. Her breathing had slowed, but her thoughts were still in a vice.

That thing was playing with me, like some kind of vicious chew toy. It's a game to him. One where only he knows the rules.

While the others pretended to be busy with Lazarus, Holbrook sat quietly beside her, patiently waiting. After several moments, he cleared his throat. "So . . . you okay?"

Ryan simultaneously shook and nodded her head.

"Want to talk about it?"

Genuine concern washed over his face—and everyone else's. She *didn't* want to talk about it. She wanted to get as far away from that thing as she could. But that was impossible.

She shook her head.

"I understand," Holbrook said, starting to rise.

"No. I mean, yes. I need to talk about this—we need to talk."

He sat back down. "What did you see?"

She brushed off the front of her pants and adjusted her shirt, mostly to collect her thoughts. "A little bit of everything. You?"

His eyes darkened. "Same."

There it was, that shared connection, the one that said 'I've stared down something too evil, too unreal to explain', something that left you forever changed. Ryan hated that he'd experienced it, too.

"Since we're sharing," Dave said, the monitor light flaring against his glasses, "Special Agent Masters paid us a visit."

Ryan's hand clenched. She tried to keep her expression even, but every fiber of her being roiled. "What did you say?"

"He's not kidding," Cori said. "Lazarus powered up all on its own. We saw him on the hologram. It was . . . him."

Ryan's nails dug into the thickest part of her palm. The elemental *had* shown her Sam during the spirit walk, and Gustav mentioned someone had followed her. Was it possible that it was Sam? That somehow he was in the mansion, able to manipulate their equipment, and terrify the others? Could he really have that much power in the afterlife?

"Did it record?" she blurted. "Show it to me."

"I think so." Dave turned his chair toward the monitor, his hands moving quickly across the keyboard. As the program launched, several windows opened showing various camera angles. Then Dave paused, keeping his eyes fixed on the screen.

"What's the matter?" Ryan asked. She moved closer, leaning over his shoulder. At the same time, Coti stood beside her, nervously chewing on her cuticle, all color drained from her face.

His mouth opened, but no words escaped. His head shook slightly, then he took a deep breath, pressed the *final* key, and then turned his head away from the screen. The recording played, the time stamp advanced, but it showed only the landing, bare and lifeless.

"I thought you said it recorded." Ryan kept her eyes on the screen.

Dave turned back. "That's not possible. It *did* record. Or at least, I thought it did." He glanced at Coti, whose eyes were fixed on the monitor. He sped through the footage, fast-forwarding several minutes until it ended. Then he restarted it.

"What happened to it?" Coti asked, lowering her hand.

"I don't know," Dave breathed. "This is the recording, but . . ." He shook his head.

"But it was there." Coti stepped around the table, her arms outstretched to the space next to the Lazarus device. "He was *right here*! We both saw him!"

Dave exhaled. "He erased it."

"How could he erase it?" Coti shouted.

"I don't know! How could he do *any* of it? How could he manipulate the system and start Lazarus? I don't know!" Dave shouted back.

"Hey," Ryan cut in. "Enough, okay?" She stepped between them, arms outstretched. "I don't know what happened here, but I *believe* you. Something's messing with us—trying to scare us, and doing a pretty good job by the looks of it. We can't let it divide us, alright?"

Coti nodded and moved back around the table. Ryan then turned to Holbrook. "You good, Doc?"

He gave a solemn nod. "I am. We need to keep going."

She knew he wasn't, none of them were. How could they be? This was new territory for all of them.

"Good," she nodded, clenching her hands. "Play it again, Dave. Just the ending."

He complied, and when the clip was done, Ryan looked around the hall. Aside from the one chaise she'd rested on, the hallway appeared as though a great storm had torn through it. But the recording showed nothing out of place. It was like a lifeless photograph. This was no ordinary house. Whatever was happening, they needed to face it as a team—if they were to survive.

The group clustered around the table. Despite the vastness of the structure, the mansion seemed to shrink around them. All that space—endless rooms, dozens of corridors—meant nothing. Their safe zone had collapsed to this small island of dim lights on the third-floor landing.

"S-Sam did that," Coti stuttered, indicating the chaos around them.

Though she believed every word that Coti said, she wasn't convinced that Sam was the cause. Ryan saw him in Purgatory, although it was the elemental in Sam's form. At least that's what she believed. Now, she wasn't so sure. Maybe it was both. Joined together to torment, tear through this house until they all went mad.

Coti shuddered, her eyes glistening in the faint light. "What if he's back, Ryan? What if he followed us here, like a ghost or something?"

Ryan pulled her friend into a hug, the woman's petite frame trembling within her arms. Of everyone here, Coti knew first-hand the psychotic nature of Sam.

Ryan released Coti, holding her by the shoulders. "I don't know if it's Sam or not. It's this house—it's twisting everything. It's trying to break us, make us see things. You can't let it. Understand? You have to be strong."

Coti nodded, trying to control her trembling. Then a slight wrinkle formed between her eyebrows. "You . . . you saw him too, didn't you? When you were in Lazarus?"

Ryan wanted to glance away from her, to the shadows at her feet. Anywhere but into those eyes full of dread. It was the same fear as the night they were trapped together in the cellar when Sam had them both cornered. The night he nearly killed Coti, just before Ryan shot him.

"You *did* see him." Coti's voice was a sharp whisper. "Why didn't you tell me?"

"Because it wasn't him," Ryan said. "This house is lying to all of us. It wants us to believe things that aren't true, and it knows what scares us. It's not him, Coti. Sam is dead. He can't get to you or me ever again."

But the moment she said it, Gustav's last words filled her mind. Someone followed her into the house, someone who didn't belong—from the outside. The entity lived here; Gloria even stated *It* made her kill herself. But it was also outside in the stable. But if it wasn't Sam or the elemental, then who was it? She rubbed her neck, trying to ease the pain that threatened to become a headache.

It didn't matter—one ghost or a thousand, they had a job to do—find Emma Harrison. Even if a spirit from the past followed her, it would have to wait. Find the girl, then deal with vengeful spirits later.

CHAPTER 25

Ryan's headache was a constant throbbing pain along the side of her temple. Sometimes rubbing her knuckles hard against the bone, making one pain more powerful than the other, helped, but not with a Lazarus headache. This one was a gold-medal winner and left lights sparkling even when she closed her eyes.

Yet, this was the only way to get the information they needed. One more time into Purgatory. One more spirit walk.

"You okay?" Coti crouched next to the chaise, hand on Ryan's arm.

The shadows darkened all around them. Even the dim glow of the Lazarus monitors did little to dispel the void. Everyone's look of apprehension made the muscles in her neck tighten. They knew what was at stake.

"You sure you want to do this again?" Dave asked.

Ryan rose from her chair and stepped into the square of cameras. "We have no choice." She knew the entity would never let them leave. She had to find a way to break its hold and to find Emma. "I can do this."

Holbrook stood outside the perimeter, unusually quiet, his hands stuffed in his pockets. His eyes held hers for a few moments, then she nodded, settled onto the floor, and crossed her legs.

The digital cameras' LED lights flared as Dave powered

them on. Coti and Colter stood behind the monitors, but Holbrook remained in place, not moving.

With every passing second, the space grew darker, and Ryan's skin prickled with anxiety. Usually, this would be a routine walk, despite the headaches and nosebleeds. But this place was anything but ordinary. It had infected this land and watched them like a living and breathing entity whose former occupants had never been allowed to leave. And she needed their help now—these wandering spirits who waited to tell their stories. There had to be at least one who knew something about Emma Harrison's story. She only needed to find that one.

"Are you ready?" Dave said.

Holbrook gazed down at her and grinned. "I'll see you soon, on the other side."

Ryan pressed her lips together and nodded. "Ready." She closed her eyes. *Help me find Emma. Any of you wandering these halls right now, help me find Emma Harrison.*

The familiar thrum of Lazarus started, the buzz starting in her thighs and hands. The grid of light fell over her, followed by the thud of the electromagnetic frequency smacking into the back of her head.

Ryan opened her eyes to the dark of the third-floor corridor. No Lazarus and no SPECTER team. Only emptiness and the never-ending cold moonlight night. She stood up and observed both ends of the hallway. Nothing but an oppressive stillness.

Facing the east corridor, she paced back through the open doorway of the Harrisons' bedroom. The curtains remained closed, and the still, cold air, mingled with the odor of blood, clung to her limbs. Nothing stirred in here, at least not in this version of Purgatory. No visions of the Harrisons, only remnants of the aftermath.

She stepped back into the empty corridor.

Where is everyone?

She moved down the hallway toward the landing, back to the place where she had started—where the unseen entity had chased her. Was the Beast waiting for her? Purgatory was its domain. It thrived off the spirits trapped here and dwelled within the gloom, waiting for its next victim. The thought of an unseen entity that hid within the shadows, waiting to attack, sent ripples of terror through her body.

Tentatively, her eyes followed the spiral staircase down to the first floor. But it wasn't the monster that she saw, but a woman with long dark hair that draped over her pajamas. And a gaping shotgun wound in the side of her head.

Their eyes met, and at that moment, the woman turned and disappeared into the atrium. Ryan bolted down the staircase, her boots slamming onto the steps in quick succession.

Please, let her still be there. For Emma's sake.

The faint moonlight cast enough light into the atrium to highlight the woman gazing out the front window. From this angle, the wound wasn't visible, and she appeared untarnished, but her skin was the familiar pale blue-white of the newly dead.

Ryan slowed as she approached. Residual energy, it seemed, wasn't bound to the place of death. Holbrook would want to know. "You must be Emily Harrison. Emma's mother."

The woman did not acknowledge her, but continued to stare out the window. Ryan slipped beside the woman, the full extent of the specter's shotgun injury fully visible. The blast had taken off most of the left side of Emily's upper skull, exposing the brain. Ryan held back a gag and turned to face the window, following the woman's gaze.

"I think something happened to my family," Emily spoke, her ethereal voice shaking.

Ryan nodded, swallowing against the spasm in her throat. "It did. That is why I'm here. I've come to help you."

The mother drew in a trembling breath. "S-Something happened." Her pale hand shook as it moved to the glass pane.

"Do you know why you came down here?" Ryan asked, keeping her eyes fixed on the window.

Emily's hand rattled against the glass. "Something happened. My family." Emily was more urgent. Her claw-like hand pounded on the pane.

Ryan reached over and touched the woman's hand, the cold sending painful chills down her own arm and into her spine. "Where's your daughter, Mrs. Harrison? Where's Emma?"

The shaking worsened, and the woman pulled her hand away. Then an unearthly wail emanated from the woman. "Noooo!" Emily clutched her fists to her shuddering chest as heart-wrenching sobs consumed her.

Ryan looked past the woman's injury and saw a mother grieving for her family. But not all were lost. "Emily, do you know where Emma is? Please, we need to find her."

"She's hiding," she said between sobs. "She is hiding from It because It wants her, too."

Ryan grabbed Emily's hand again. "Wait! Your daughter is alive?"

The woman still refused to look at her but continued to stare out the window. "Not for long."

"Please," Ryan said sharply. "Where. Is. She? Where's your daughter?"

The woman again pulled her cold hand from Ryan's grasp and pointed a bony finger against the glass. Ryan followed her gaze.

"That little boy knows," Emily whispered as she pointed into the dark night.

Ryan's brow furrowed. "Little boy?" She glanced out the window but saw only darkness.

In that instant, a horrendous wail resounded throughout the building. It knew what Emily had told her. Emily's eye grew wide, and she glanced up the staircase in terror. With one furtive look toward Ryan, she dissipated into nothing.

The house rumbled and the rafters shook as the elemental roared. Thundering footsteps resounded from above her. It was coming.

Ryan looked out the window, trying to see where the spirit of Emily had pointed. Where she knew that the child had hidden. Her heart raced as the thundering footsteps grew louder. She willed herself to see the boy, but the darkness of Purgatory kept him out of view.

Purgatory.

Ryan looked at the door. She was a spirit here. Maybe . . . Taking a deep breath, she closed her eyes and ran straight through the closed front door.

The dense substance of the wood coursed through her body, every molecule passing through hers. She was on the other side in a single breath. The motion was so seamless that it unbalanced her, and she fell to her knees on the driveway pavement, feeling the full impact. Pain shot through her legs.

She looked toward the door. The laws of physics in Purgatory made no sense—something she and Holbrook would have to unravel later, assuming she wasn't ripped apart from the elemental first. She could sense the creature storming through the house—its fury pulsing through the walls, the very atmosphere. Its hatred seeped outward, like blood soaking through cloth. And the Beast knew Ryan was spirit walking, looking for Emma. And she knew it was getting closer.

Ryan pulled herself up and tried to sprint forward, but something was wrong. One leg dragged, like it was stuck in mud. Her next step locked, throwing her off balance, and she crumpled forward, landing hard on her hands and knees. The driveway surface gave way, not like gravel or stone, but like flesh. Yielding, then tightening.

The ground rippled and slithered with purpose. She pulled at her limbs. A horrifying entity coursed through it—through the vines that wrapped tighter around her. They didn't just want to trap her. They *wanted* her.

Every time she struggled, the pull grew stronger. And deeper. Her heart pounded, but it didn't matter. Her lungs strained for air—but it was futile. She fought for breath, for movement, anything—but it was useless. Panic rose in her chest, then curdled into something worse: resignation.

The creature's shrieks echoed through the mansion. Not with rage or hunger, but with delight. She belonged to It now.

Ryan squeezed her eyes shut. She sensed it slithering beneath the surface, slipping along the vines, moving in for the final kill. It wanted her to feel this. To know that she had lost. She clawed at the ground, but her fingers met only shifting matter. She blinked sweat from her lashes. Not sweat—tears.

"I'm sorry, Emma," she rasped softly as she was pulled beneath the asphalt.

A hand seized her upper arm.

Ryan gasped as her momentum reversed, as if caught mid-fall. The force lifted her through the suffocating sludge that was to be her grave and dragged her across the pavement toward the shadowy front step of the mansion.

"No." Ryan tried to struggle. "I have to save…."

A child's voice replied above her. Calm. Unfamiliar. "You can't go there."

Small fingers, impossibly strong, continued to drag her away from the entity, away from Emma. A child shouldn't have the strength to pull her out of the sludge, let alone to break the bonds of whatever had held her. Her body scraped along the ground, then eased to a stop on the cold grass.

Small hands moved to her face, his touch stiff like wax. Nerves fired along her spine, a deep jolt that made her twitch. Purgatory blurred the boundaries between life and spirit, and sensations here came without rules. Everything felt too vivid, as if her nerves were directly wired into the skin of the world.

"Don't go any farther from the mansion or you will die," the child said, his voice a soft, hollow whisper.

She lifted her head, breath ragged, pushing herself up on trembling knees. The boy looked no more than ten years old, his short blonde hair dripping onto the shoulder straps of faded denim coveralls.

"You." Her voice sounded dull and paper-thin in the vacuum of this place. "Are you the one that's been following me? The one Gustav told me about?"

The boy nodded, sending small droplets of water across his shoulders.

"You can't walk far from your machine. Its power keeps your spirit alive in this place. You have to go back. You're in terrible danger."

"Danger?" she said, every word getting heavier, harder to breathe. "You mean . . . the shadow thing?"

"Yes. The Beast knows what you know. It is with all of you now. Go back."

"What do you mean *with* all of us?"

His gaze didn't waver. "One of your friends is infected. You have to go back now."

She turned her head toward the mansion door, then back to him. "But I can't leave you like this. It's not safe here with that thing. Come back with me."

His cold hand touched hers. "It won't let me inside, and I must stay out here. I have to stay with her." Their eyes locked, his pupils darkening. That was all the confirmation Ryan needed.

"Okay." Her hand grasped his as she nodded. "Thank you."

He nodded. "You'll see me soon." And then he was gone.

CHAPTER 26

In a flash of white, the world collapsed into a cavity of darkness. Purgatory dissolved as Ryan toppled sideways, eyes flying open. Pain detonated at the back of her skull, like being hit with a baseball bat.

"Ahhh!" Ryan yelled, her shoulder slamming into the ground—the thrumming of mini-Lazarus ebbing away. Coti crouched beside her.

"Something's wrong," Ryan winced, her vision swimming in a pool of flashing stars. She tried to stand, but her legs buckled again, and Coti caught her.

Colter rushed forward, grasping Ryan's other arm. "You need to lie down."

"No. Something's really wrong."

Ryan forced herself upright and lurched to one side, where Colter steadied her.

The room was dim, but the active monitors provided enough reference points. That was enough.

"Dave," she called out.

"Right here, boss."

Ryan staggered to the table until she bumped into it, one hand catching the surface to steady herself, Colter and Coti holding onto her arms.

"Did you see anything on the playback, Dave?"

"I got a glimpse of something, but not a lot."

She swayed from the pain, the taste of blood hitting her throat. Coti dabbed Ryan's nose, stopping the flow of bleeding.

"I think Emma's alive," she coughed, "and I know where she is."

She jerked when the watch buzzed violently on her wrist. The face lit up in a blinding flash of white.

Bang!

Colter dropped away, releasing her arm as a thunderous crack split the night.

Ryan hit the floor, head tucked and arms up to protect her face. Training and adrenaline surged through every fiber. "Coti!" Grasping her friend's wrist, she yanked her under the table. They scrambled into the dark, and she reached for Dave's pant leg, hauling him down beside them. The wheelchair toppled, crashing to the floor, and Dave curled into himself, protecting his head.

Another flash. Then another.

Bang! Bang!

Ryan shoved the table over as a barrier as monitors cracked and clattered to the floor. Coti screamed, her body crumpled into a ball, hands over her ears. Ryan huddled beside her, shielding both her and Dave.

The house had turned into a war zone.

Heart pounding like a jackhammer, she reached for her weapon.

The holster was empty. Ryan desperately searched along the floor, but her weapon was gone.

Okay, new plan.

Ryan clenched her teeth and leaned toward Dave. "We have to move. Now!"

Grabbing Coti's trembling arm, she pulled her toward the

edge of the overturned table as more gunfire erupted behind them. Coti screamed and again curled into a ball, whimpering in the dark.

"Coti, I won't let anything happen to you." Coti remained near catatonic.

"Hey, kiddo," Dave whispered. "Focus on me. Focus on my voice."

Coti continued to whimper, her body shaking violently.

"I'm here, Coti." Dave's soft voice continued. "I won't leave you, okay?"

Her cries subsided. "Okay." She sobbed.

"I've got you. Don't let go of my hand." Coti squeezed Ryan's hand.

"On the count of three, Dave. One, Two, Three . . ."

With Dave crawling close behind, Coti and Ryan plunged down to the second-floor landing and ducked through the nearest open door they could find. Darkness swallowed them. More gunshots rang out as they crouched against the far wall.

"What the hell is going on?" Dave whispered, his voice shaking.

"You okay?" Ryan asked, patting his leg.

"Yeah, I think so," he said. "It's Coti I'm worried about." The woman sat next to them, rocking softly, still clutching Ryan's hand.

"Coti? You still with us?"

Coti looked up, her brow furrowed. "Ryan. W-What's . . . who . . . ?" Thankful to hear her voice, Ryan eased her hand from the vice-like grip.

"Long story short, one of the team is infected."

"You mean under the control of the elemental?" Dave asked.

"Yes."

"Y-You think the shooter is one of us . . .?" Coti gasped.

"Wait," Dave said. "Where's Doc?"

Another gunshot echoed down the hallway—closer. Ryan turned toward the sound.

Doc!

Staying low, she crawled toward where a faint line of light oozed from under the door. Pressing her ear to the cold wood, she listened for any movement.

"I thought Doc was with the sheriff," Coti whispered. "Where did the shot come from?"

"I'm not sure." Ryan suppressed a smile at Coti's clear-headed thinking. "And not to add fuel, but my pistol is missing."

"Well, my money's on Sheriff Watson," Dave replied. "What if he shot Doc?" Ryan didn't want to consider the possibility.

The hallway beyond remained deathly quiet. No footfalls. The shooting had stopped, and whoever had the gun now knew that the three of them had disappeared.

She turned her head, whispering to the darkness. "Coti, can you take Dave to the back of the room and keep him safe? I need to find Doc."

"Definitely, and Ryan?"

"Yeah."

"Be careful."

She heard their soft shuffling across the floor. Then, Ryan's heart lurched.

"Shhhh," she hissed. "Don't move . . ." Someone was moving methodically along the antique rugs. Old floorboards offered the slightest squeak with each shift of weight. Ryan held her breath, watching as a shadow moved past the door and then paused.

They were listening.

She flashed a glance through the dark toward Coti and Dave, unsure they could see her, and held a finger up to her lips. Ryan bit her lip to not make a sound. Her hand instinctively moved to the empty holster at her hip. Anyone could have taken her weapon while she was in Lazarus. She cursed herself for not asking Dave or Coti to hold onto it; they had been the closest when she spirit walked.

The floorboard creaked again as the sounds of the shooter passed the door and continued down the hall. She turned once more and held up her hand. She hoped they could see her and smiled when they replied with a tiny tap on the floor. Nodding, she turned back to the door.

For the moment, they were safe, but she had to lure the shooter away. Pressing her ear to the door, she heard the steps receding down the corridor. It could be a trap, luring her into false security, but this wasn't about her now.

Swallowing hard, she slowly turned the door handle. It clicked softly, making her heart almost burst. She held her breath, ready to defend her team if the elemental came rushing through the door. She carefully pulled the door open a crack and peered down the hall. An unknown shadow continued to move away. Soon, he'd reach the end of the hall and head back.

Ryan steadied her breathing. It was now or never. *Okay, on three. One, Two . . .*

Boom!

She lurched backward as the sound of a door being kicked open echoed down the corridor. She glanced back at the others huddled in the darkness. Then, she rose to her feet and waited, visualizing her flight.

The hinge swung silently, and she peered into the darkened corridor as the hammering of her heart deafened anything that she could hear in the hallway. Nothing moved in the faint moonlight that shone across the landing where the staircase spiraled up and down. Perhaps the shooter had gone back down the stairs to a lower level.

Boom!

Ryan threw open the door and sprinted down the hallway toward the second-floor landing and flew up the staircase. Her only hope was to find a weapon she could use. If it was one of her people, she needed to subdue, not kill, if possible. Hopefully, he wouldn't suspect her of going back to their point of origin.

Reaching the third floor, she eased her flight, moving methodically, silently across the carpet. The monitor table remained overturned. Camera tripods lay strewn about the floor. Only mini-Lazarus had survived.

She scrambled to the floor and felt among the wreckage. One of the monitors had shattered. Wires stretched like snakes across the ground, and the tripods crisscrossed one another throughout the place. Ryan had hoped her weapon hadn't been taken, that she'd only lost it somewhere in the mess. But she knew that wasn't likely.

Her fingers brushed against the leg of one tripod—heavy enough for a defense. She pulled it closer and unscrewed the camera from the base.

"Ryan," a voice whispered from behind her, fingers touching her shoulder. She braced her knees and swung the tripod hard over her shoulder. It whistled through the air, barely missing its target.

"Whoa!" Colter ducked, landing hard on his back with a grunt. "Ahh—easy!" He raised his hands in surrender. Ryan flipped over, breathing hard, still gripping the tripod. "Where's your weapon?"

"I don't have it. It's gone," he said, voice strained. "Doc's the one who shot me."

"What?" She scowled as she scrambled to her feet, brandishing her weapon. "That's not possible. He'd never . . ."

Colter rolled to his right side, pulling down the collar of his shirt, revealing a fresh bleeding wound along his shoulder. "Look. He fired when I tried to stop him—he raised the gun at you. He's lost his mind."

She tried to process. Holbrook didn't even *like* guns. Ryan lowered the tripod and helped Colter to his feet.

"This can't be happening," she said. "He must have taken our guns while I was inside Lazarus." Ryan paced slowly across the floor, shaking her head. How could Holbrook have gotten infected? *I've been with him almost the entire time.* No black-eye possession like Chad. No shifts in behavior. No warning.

"I told you," Colter said, cradling his arm, "he's lost his mind."

Then came the unmistakable sound of a gun cocking. A jolt buzzed her wrist—pulsing red with a single green blip. Colter froze, eyes widening in dread.

Ryan didn't need to turn around. She knew. It wouldn't be Matt Holbrook, only the puppet with an evil master pulling the strings.

"I know you can hear me, Matt," she said, turning slowly, her voice hollow in the long corridors of the mansion.

Holbrook stood on the landing, gun aimed at her head. His face was both familiar and alien. Eyes vacant. Mouth slick. Something else resided there now. Whispering lies, sinking in when no one was watching. Twisting him from the inside.

"You don't have to do this, Doc." The buzz of the watch intensified.

Holbrook said nothing. A faint glint of silver flashed in his dark eyes. The same cold, dead stare as Chad Harrison when he'd walked into his parents' room and into the interrogation room.

Tilting his head slightly, Holbrook's finger slipped onto the trigger.

"Doc, don't . . ."

His finger tightened—A whistle cut through the air.

Thud.

Holbrook crumpled onto the carpet, the gun landing beside him.

Ryan blinked at Coti standing on the landing behind him, wide-eyed and trembling, holding a tripod in her hand.

CHAPTER 27

Ryan watched from the front door of the atrium as Colter finished tying Holbrook to a chair from the dining hall. Coti, ever resourceful, found enough duct tape to secure Holbrook at the ankles, wrists, and across the chest.

Holbrook didn't resist, nor did he seem to care. Since regaining consciousness, he hadn't said a word. He just sat there, staring, directly at Ryan with a cold, dark gaze that never blinked.

Ryan kept one hand on her weapon. The last thing she'd ever want to do was to shoot a co-worker—a friend. Did he know how much the silence unnerved her?

Colter stepped back. "Okay, that should hold him."

Dave, now safe in his wheelchair, rolled away from Holbrook. "I don't like this. What's wrong with him?"

Ryan took a deep breath, exhaling slowly. "Same thing that happened to Chad. Possession. And it's been happening since this mansion was built. Maybe even longer."

Pushing away from the wall, she stepped toward Holbrook. Hungry eyes watched her, tracked her. They didn't belong to the intelligent scientist who was her friend, but a cold and calculating beast that was plotting its next move. Was he gone forever? How much of *Holbrook* was left? Her stomach clenched at the thought.

She turned to face the remainder of her team. "That

thing that has trapped us—it's feeding off the spirits here. The Harrisons. The Treadwells. It needed Ms. Barrister to die by the gardener's hand, that little boy to drown, and Gustav to be murdered." She crouched before Matt. "You feed on death. Sorrow. Pain. And now, you need Emma Harrison to die too, don't you? And you want us to die here. Because if we don't," she leaned closer, "you'll shrivel into nothing."

A flicker tugged at the corner of Holbrook's mouth. Thin. Icy. Intentional. Then it was gone. Replaced by the same soulless stare.

"So, what do we do?" Colter said. "The house is still locked up. And Holbrook's . . . *gone.*"

Ryan turned her head toward the others. They were not safe with Holbrook. Even if they made it out, he wasn't in control. She knew the moment they untied him, he'd attack. The sheriff was right. Holbrook was gone.

Shifting her eyes back to Matt, she swallowed the lump rising in her throat. He was still in there somewhere, but how could she reach him? How do you break the spiritual bonds of an elemental?

Coti moved beside her. "What are we gonna do?"

"I don't know." Ryan stood and turned away.

"This is Doc, Ryan. He'd never hurt us. We *have* to help him."

Ryan spun on her, her eyes glistening. "I'm out of ideas. So, if you've got anything, please share it with me."

Coti flinched, but didn't answer.

"What about Lazarus?" Dave said, wheeling into the huddle. "What if you can go in and *find* him. Doc has to be in there *somewhere.* Do a session with *him* . . ." He nodded toward Holbrook, "while he's in the circle."

Ryan met Doc's cold gaze as he scanned the group. Then, she crouched and stared back at him, gently placing her hands on his.

"Hold on, Matt. I'm coming to get you."

They worked quickly—moving and resetting the equipment from the third floor. Once Dave had Lazarus ready, Ryan took her place on the floor across from Holbrook. She was surprised he didn't struggle against the restraints. He knew what they were doing, yet he didn't appear concerned. That, more than anything, worried her.

Other than the few minutes of setup noise, silence fell between them. Ryan didn't look away. She studied him in the dim light, letting herself *feel* what he'd become. She needed to face it squarely, no matter how much it twisted her stomach. This creature wasn't Matt. Not the man who quoted weird nineteenth-century chemists and wore bad cologne on purpose. This was something else. Something ancient, calculating, and filled with infinite hatred.

This *thing* had taken Chad—she would die before it took Matt.

This was her enemy. This was her serial killer. This was an infection that needed to be eradicated, an evil that needed to be imprisoned in the dark depths of hell so it could never hurt another soul again.

She had to find a way to stop it, or Matt would be lost forever. She studied It. The elemental that believed it had beaten them all. But somewhere, in Purgatory, she had to find a way to stop it. Otherwise, Matt would be lost forever.

"You ready?" Colter asked.

Ryan never broke her contact with the creature. "Do it."

The familiar pulse of blue light flickered across the floor, surrounding Holbrook's chair and the perimeter. Usually, she closed her eyes before the grid dropped. But not this time. She kept her gaze locked on Holbrook's eyes. Looking for the Matt she knew.

A second before the flash, she let her eyes close.

No mansion this time—only an endless abyss of dark mist that clung to her skin and seeped deep into her bones. It coiled around her limbs and tugged at her skin. Every breath resounded in her ears like hollow roars.

The fog swirled around her legs and knees. The ground crunched beneath her boots, like loose gravel buried under ash. The fog split with each step, then it would suck back in again.

"Matt!" she shouted out, her voice absorbed by the fog like a sponge, then returned, muffled and from every direction.

This place wasn't the mansion. It wasn't even close. Wherever Lazarus had sent her this time, it was colder, emptier. She swept her hand before her, pushing through the tangible gray mass.

"Matt. Can you hear me?"

The fog thickened, seeping into her lungs. It blurred all sense of direction—up and down melted into one suffocating expanse. Every step a risk: a sudden drop, or worse—something hidden within the mist.

Something like *him*.

She called Matt's name again and again. The pressing mist was so palpable that she could no longer breathe without choking. She covered her mouth with her sleeve. Then, the toe of her boot hit something solid, and she reached out. Her hands shot out, and she sensed the rough edges of a door and a cold metal handle. Gripping it hard, she twisted. Locked. Of course.

Yet, it was the only solid thing in this gray void. That had to mean something.

Pressing her forehead to the door, she closed her eyes, listening. The fog wrapped tighter around her throat. She coughed, doubling over, then slammed her palm against the wood.

"Matt! Can you hear me?" She coughed against the fog slipping into her lungs again.

With open palms, she pounded on the door and then yanked the handle again, but it still didn't give way. She stepped back, exhaled, and closed her eyes.

Come on, evaluate the situation. There's one door, Alice. Where's the key?

As the fog pressed in, she leaned back, pivoted on her left leg, and kicked the door with all her strength. The black door shattered—violently, impossibly—into a thousand pieces, revealing a stark, sterile room with floor-to-ceiling, sky-blue ceramic tiles that gleamed under harsh overhead lights, like a hospital bathroom. Not one shadow remained in this space.

And there, curled on the floor in the center of the room, was Holbrook. He lay on his side, knees drawn to his chest, arms wrapped around his legs, his head buried. He didn't move. Not even when the door exploded open. Ryan rushed forward and dropped to her knees beside him.

"Matt," she whispered, placing a hand on his shoulder. He flinched, curling tighter into a fetal position. A pained screech escaped him as she tried again.

"Hey, Matt, it's me. Ryan."

Every touch made him cry out and inch farther away. "Please, Doc." Her voice cracked. "P-please, look at me."

Nothing got through to him in this echoing, bright chamber of misery. Ryan finally crawled over until her body hovered over him. She lowered her body, arms locking around him, her legs over his. She held tight until he couldn't pull away.

The groans that crept from his throat tore at her heart, but she couldn't stop, not until she had him in a full embrace. She rested her head against his and closed her eyes.

Just like Lexi, she thought. When they fought as kids, wrestling on the ground in knock-down, drag-out fights, they would hold each other until they both stopped struggling—this was how they made up. Their parents made them hold each other, for what sometimes felt like hours, until they forgave each other.

We held on until we were friends again. Well, Matt was going to be her 'friend again' if it killed her. If this had been Lexi, she'd have kissed her cheek over and over again until she finally gave up and said *I love you.* She wasn't about to do that with Matt, but she would hold him until he remembered who he was and what they needed to do.

"I'm not letting you go, Matt," she whispered in his ear. "Come back to me."

He whimpered, trying to wrench free for what seemed like hours. Though her muscles ached, Ryan held him tight, continuing to whisper to him.

"I'll never leave you, Matt."

Slowly, the muscles along his spine eased beneath her touch. As his muscles relaxed, his head drifted against her shoulder.

"Mills?" he croaked. "Ryan . . . is it really you?"

"I don't know anybody else who'd be doing this to you right now." A hoarse laugh escaped his lips as she lightly stroked his hair. She loosened her grip around his torso and unhooked her legs from his.

Then she heard it.

A faint chittering—wet, insectile.

Ryan glanced to the upper corner of the room where a black mass bloomed and devoured the light like a living void. The light flickered, dimmed, and then vanished as the shadows expanded outward in waves.

Her hand clamped around Holbrook's forearm. "I don't mean to rush you, but we need to leave. Now. Get on your feet."

Holbrook tried to stand, but his legs buckled. Ryan jumped up, wrapped her arms around Matt's torso, and dragged him across the tiles toward the exit. A chill descended into the room as the darkness pulsated closer. She didn't need to look. She sensed it reaching for her like a mass of attacking spiders.

The lights flickered as the elemental pulled its way across the room. Tendrils of black spread across the walls and floor, stretching like cracks in reality, and sucking every bit of warmth from the air.

It pulled at her with everything it had. Not only her body, but her *being*. A gravitational force, ancient and hungry, drawing her toward its gaping maw. Lightbulbs exploded, sending shards of glass across the floor. The elemental roared—no longer a single sound, but a cacophony of every voice it had ever silenced throughout the millennia of its existence. The spirits within its darkness screamed and reached out for help, only to be pulled back into its depths as it lunged at Ryan and Matt.

She stumbled toward the still doorway, still open, still reachable. But every step was more difficult than the last as its power grew stronger.

Her boot slipped, and Holbrook clung tighter to Ryan's arm as the floor behind them crumbled and vanished. She was weakening, her legs shaking under the strain. It took every ounce of strength to keep them from falling into the creature's waiting jaws.

"He does not belong to you!" she screamed at the mass.

A coil of black lashed forward between Ryan's legs, twisting around her ankle. Ryan gasped, falling to one knee, pulling Holbrook with her. But Matt caught the edge of the doorframe and latched on, wrapping his other arm around her shoulder.

"Hold on to me!" he yelled.

She locked both arms around him. The creature pulled harder, lifting her into the air, stretching her body taut. This thing had had her once before, in the stables. It had tasted her fear and, from that moment, it wanted *her*. It invaded her soul, creeping through her body like frostbite and venom. She screamed, clinging tighter to Holbrook, and its hunger pressed tighter.

It *knew* her.

It wanted her.

She screamed and squeezed her eyes shut.

Then—silence. No roaring wind. No howling. Not even Holbrook's voice. Only dead silence.

Ryan hung suspended in the stillness, like a broken marionette. Then a single voice broke the quiet. Familiar. Unwanted. One that made Ryan's skin crawl.

Not the elemental's voice.

His.

A sound she never wanted to hear again.

It wasn't real, she thought. It *couldn't* be.

But the house, *this house,* made it real.

A figure stood in front of her. Mere inches from her face. She felt its warmth touching her forehead, her cheeks, her closed eyelids.

Her lips.

The elemental's weightless pull faded, replaced by the coarse press of a hard surface. Coarse and dull. Ryan had been here before. A place she'd vowed never to see again.

This was everything therapy tried to control. Every imagined scenario come to life—head pounding, body shaking and immobile from the drug *he'd* given her. Musty air, flickering candlelight creating shadows that danced along the low ceiling. Everything horribly familiar. So, too, was the sound of his voice.

A single finger traced along her jawline and curved behind her ear. A whisper of warm breath grazed the side of her neck.

"Once again upon the stair," he whispered. Ryan's chest shuddered with a broken sob. "I saw the man who wasn't there."

It's a lie. This isn't real. Sam was dead. She killed him over a year ago. Two bullets, point blank. But here he was. His presence, his rhyme, his scent, dredged up by the house and the thing inside it.

Tears flowed from the corners of her eyes. She couldn't move—drugged again in this nightmare memory, pinned in place by her own terror. Whatever twisted necromancy spell he believed in, it was always about her—her abilities, her powers—and he'd planned it for years. Just so he could control the dead.

He moved around the head of the slab, looming over her now. His hands rested around her throat—lightly, teasing. But his eyes had turned pitch black. Not Sam's. Not anymore.

"He took me to the earth today," Sam murmured, continuing the rhyme. "And now, oh how, he carried me away."

The elemental knew everything about that night. Every word. Every violation. His thumb gently swept away a tear at the corner of her eye. "Shh. There's no need for that. I'm here now."

She shook her head. "No, you're not. You're dead. You're only a memory dug out of my brain by that thing keeping us hostage."

He smiled, the white of his teeth like fangs in dim candlelight. "You could believe that if you want. Or. . ." he said, raising his eyebrows and then suddenly, jumping with the agility of a cat onto the cement slab, straddling her, "you could believe I am really here with you, following your every move."

Ryan's stomach turned at the sight. Sam was shirtless, like he'd been that night. Muscles rippled under smooth skin tattooed in so many places. And the skull with the emerald eyes, the one that peeked out above the waistband of his jeans. The same one the spirits of his victims had warned her about so many times.

Yet, now, the skull opened its mouth, spewing black steam. Sam shifted his weight. With one hand pressed onto the floor beside her ear, Sam leaned over, his face inches away from hers, his oil black eyes boring into her.

"Perhaps, the spells that I worked—the years of work that I put into them—were all for this: to be with you forever. Did you ever think of that?"

With his free hand, he slid a finger along her collarbone and down the front of her V-neck shirt. Ryan clenched her jaw. *No. Not again. Not this time.* She willed her limbs to move, her fingers, anything. Nothing. She was trapped in the dark basement, with the closeness of Sam pressed against her.

"Somebody, please wake me up," she begged, hot tears spilling down her cheeks.

"What was that?" Sam pressed closer, his finger moving further down her shirt, the bristle of his face scraping against her cheek.

Ryan forced her fingers into a weak clench. "Get me out of here, please."

"Nobody can help you." Sam chuckled. "You are mine."

Don't let go, Ryan.

Her heart jolted, and her eyes flew open. That wasn't Sam. That was—Matt! Before Sam, she'd been with Holbrook. This room, the dark basement, the smell of burning wax—this wasn't real.

Keep holding onto me.

"I won't let go," she whispered back.

"You're not going anywhere," Sam snarled, reeling back, his face contorting into a twisted expression. Hands closed hard around her throat.

Terror filled her eyes as she struggled to breathe. Stars formed, and she felt her life draining, leaving her. She was dying.

Close your eyes, Ryan.

She gave in to Matt's voice, trusting him, even when Sam ripped at her shirt. Suddenly, the pressure of the slab beneath her gave way, and she fell backward, but another hand caught her.

"I've got you!" Matt said.

Ryan opened her eyes. The cellar and Sam had vanished. Only Matt faced her now. "I've got you," he whispered again. Holding her tight, they stepped through the gaping doorway.

Behind them, the seething elemental roared, and its ever-growing dark force filled the room. It rushed toward them just as the door that Ryan had shattered with a kick reappeared and slammed shut, sealing the parasitic creature inside.

Ryan and Matt tumbled into the dark fog of the empty void—momentarily free, breathless, and holding each other. The black door had sealed them away from the room, and the door handle had vanished. Nothing remained but the void.

With Matt's arm still around her, Ryan filled her lungs and shouted into the cold abyss:

"Get us out of here!"

CHAPTER 28

Ryan teetered backward when her eyes snapped open and the laser grid vanished. The pounding in her skull barely registered because the moment she met Holbrook's eyes and saw that faint, genuine smile, she knew: he was free.

Sam's phantom touch still undulated under her skin, but she shook it off before turning to Coti, Dave, and Colter.

"Are we good?" Coti called, the monitor's glow casting her face in blue.

Ryan nodded. "Yeah." Although Ryan suspected she'd need ten years of therapy after this.

"Excuse me," Holbrook rasped from where he sat bound in the dark. "Would someone mind getting me out of this."

Ryan smirked. "You all there, Doc?"

"Thanks to you." The edge of his smile reappeared.

Coti and Dave rushed to him, but Ryan caught Colter's arm. "You guys see to Doc. Sheriff, I need you with me right now."

Ryan barely waited for Colter's nod before pulling him toward the front door. So much had happened since the drowned boy had stopped her and stopped her from leaving the mansion during her spirit walk. The child had been right—straying too far from Lazarus would have killed her. But because of him and Emma's mother, she may have uncovered the girl's hiding place.

Ryan released a sigh of relief as she turned the knob that had been locked all night. The door opened wide, and she smiled as the first rays of light kissed the morning sky. She inhaled the fresh dawn air, breathing deep. The elemental's hold was weakening.

She stepped out the door with Colter at her side, her eyes locking on the old well house. "I know where Emma Harrison is," she said. "Radio dispatch. Get Agent Finn and the rest of the FBI out here now."

She didn't wait for Colter's reply. Cool air rushed past her ears as she pushed away from the front stoop and took off.

"Where are you going?" he shouted.

"To find her before it's too late. Tell them to meet me there."

Ryan trusted Colter to radio for backup and for Coti and Dave to watch over Holbrook. There was no time to waste. Light tickled the edge of the horizon as her boots pounded through wet grass. She ran toward the place with the strongest tug—toward the boy.

The same little boy who said he needed to stay outside, and now Ryan knew why.

Everything around her blurred. She gave in to the visions that swirled in her mind. It was the way she let it happen. She was free of the mansion but not the spirits that came with it. For the moment, they were freed and needed to tell her what had happened.

Emma had run here that night because this was the safest place to be. She knew it because the boy who had died here in 1908 had shown her before. The little girl had played with him so many times, and now, he took Ryan to this play, down the path that Emma had run that night. She'd been terrified; she knew something bad had happened. The only thing Emma understood was that little Robert Allen Forrester, her friend, said she needed to run and hide, so she did.

The girl had run toward the wellhouse and fell to her knees where the bricks were loose on the south side of the wellhouse foundation. And Robert had stayed with Emma until Ryan had needed his help tonight.

Just as he had saved Emma from death, he'd saved Ryan from dying in Purgatory. Now, he needed her help—for Emma. Ryan dropped to her knees, the wet grass soaking through her pants, clawing at the debris until her hands hit stone.

Yes!

There, in the crumbling mortar—a gap—barely large enough for a child to slip through. The secret hiding place that only Robert and Emma knew.

Ryan flicked on her flashlight, angling the beam into the darkness. Robert's presence wrapped around her thoughts. *Keep her safe, Robert. Tell her I'm coming.*

Through Robert's eyes, she could see that the tunnel snaked downward, under the building, and into the bottom of the dry well. Emma was there. Sick, cold, and running out of time.

With her heart hammering in her ears, Ryan turned. Colter stood by his SUV, radio to his mouth, eyes tracking her every move. She waved her flashlight, then jammed the flashlight between her teeth, and dropped to her belly, shoving herself headfirst into the cold tunnel.

The crumbling wall gave way, and she dragged herself along the muddy tunnel. Roots clawed at her sleeves and tangled her hair. She ignored the claustrophobic press of the dirt ceiling against her shoulders, inching forward slowly. Her breath hissed around the flashlight clenched between her teeth. One slip, and the wall might bury her alive.

Please stay with me, Robert, she pleaded in her mind. *Guide me just a little longer.*

Somewhere, in the dark, a frightened heartbeat waited—small and fading. Walking on her elbows, Ryan continued forward, inches at a time, over rock and mud through the dark cavern, deeper and deeper.

The tunnel snaked to the left another ten or twelve feet, shifting from mud to slick rock until it began to open. Then the beam fell on a small bare foot, pale skin, and toes caked in dirt. Ryan's voice caught in her throat when she touched the girl's ice-cold skin.

"Emma."

Only the echo of trickling water against the stone answered. The tunnel walls snagged her clothes as she pulled herself into the open base of the well, but she paused when the light caught a pale face near the far wall—a boy, hair dripping, knees tucked tight to his chest.

Robert Forrester.

He appeared as he had outside the mansion: waterlogged overalls, blank, patient eyes. Waiting. Watching. Keeping vigil beside Emma's still body on the flagstones.

The girl's hair was matted and damp. The muddy nightgown clung to her petite frame, curled into a fetal position for warmth, her legs tucked under the gown. Ryan pulled herself into the chamber and reached toward the girl. But the girl didn't move or awaken.

"Is she alive?" Ryan whispered to the little boy who sat in the dark of the well.

Robert didn't speak. He only held her gaze with wide, eyes set in a waxy, pale face. He waited like a loyal friend. There was nothing more he could do than keep Emma company while her strength slipped away. He watched as his friend gradually developed hypothermia, and he stayed with her until she rested her head on the ground and fell asleep.

Ryan's throat burned as she pressed closer to the child. "Emma? Can you hear me?" She touched the girl's shoulder and then moved her hand to her back. The tiny ribs barely moved, but at least they *did* move. Her trembling, muddy fingers gently touched the child's throat. A pulse still thrummed, faint.

A stinging heat blurred Ryan's vision, no matter how hard she tried to push it away. Robert watched motionless, save for the constant drip of water from his hair. Ryan positioned herself over Emma to protect and provide body heat. She wanted to hold the child in her arms, but moving her could create more injury before the paramedics arrived. She placed her head on the stone next to Emma's and looked up at Robert.

"Thank you for watching over her," she whispered. "I'm sorry for what happened to you."

Robert finally shifted, scooting his bottom across the flagstones until he sat by her side. He laid his small hand over Ryan's, where it cupped Emma's shoulder. The cold of it made goosebumps rise on the back of her arm. Robert's face remained expressionless, but his eyes moved to Emma's still head. Ryan let her head rest back, and she watched Robert like this in the dark, the three of them alone as she warmed the child's small body with her own.

A light broke through the well above them with the tearing wood, breaking boards. Sunlight poured into the mouth, washing the cold stone walls with gold.

But Robert didn't move or acknowledge the sounds above them.

"Agent Mills!" a voice echoed down the shaft.

Sirens wailed faintly in the distance, crawling closer. Flashlight beams stabbed through the darkness as bobbing figures peered into the pit.

Coti's voice sounded from above her. "Ryan!"

"Special Agent Mills," another voice called out, certain and sharp. "Hold tight."

Ryan raised her head, squinting into the light. "I have her! She's alive. She needs paramedics now!"

"We've got them en route," Agent Finn said.

She dropped her gaze again, but Robert was gone. His lonely, sad eyes no longer watched them. Just the cold stone and the girl he'd helped save. Maybe he was still near, hidden in the shadows, satisfied that the living could finish what he'd started.

Ryan pressed her head back against Emma and felt the girl twitch. A weak moan came from the child's throat. Ryan nearly sobbed with relief.

"I've got you, baby girl," she breathed into the girl's damp hair. "You're safe now. I'm not leaving you." Ryan's hand gently closed around Emma's tiny fingers. "I promised your mama, and I keep my promises."

CHAPTER 29

Ryan pulled the FBI jacket over her shoulders and watched the paramedics load Emma into the back of the ambulance. The sun had just crested the mountain ridgeline, but its warmth hadn't reached the mansion or dried the mud clinging to Ryan's arms. She shivered beneath the jacket, exhausted, but stood tall, proud of the insignia and what it meant: Emma was safe.

Agent Finn, with his slick hair and confident smirk, approached with his hands on his hips. "Well, I had my doubts, but you and your team pulled it off. You actually found her."

Holbrook drifted closer, a quiet anchor at her shoulder, gently flicking a small speck of dried dirt from Ryan's cheek. "Why would you ever doubt such an exceptional team, Agent Finn?"

Finn chuckled, raising his palms in surrender. "I'll never doubt it again, and I'll keep your number on file for next time."

He turned to leave, but Ryan's mind raced ahead of her voice. It was reckless—maybe stupid after everything they'd survived—but the thought wouldn't let go. Holbrook and the others would try to stop her, but she had to try. She lunged after Finn and caught him by the shoulder, tugging him aside out of earshot.

Finn cocked an eyebrow. "Need something else? Maybe a shower?" The smirk was enough to make her almost regret asking him.

"Is Chad Harrison still in custody at the Currant Falls Precinct?"

His grin slipped. "He's slated for transfer to Montpelier tomorrow."

"I need to speak to him one more time."

He frowned. "Why? You found the girl. Case closed, right?"

Ryan's jaw tightened, and she balled a fist. He didn't need to know why. "It's SPECTER business. Classified."

Finn exhaled, studying her face for a second too long before sighing. "You've got an hour. Don't make me regret this."

"You sure about this?" Holbrook stared through the one-way glass at the young man shackled in the interrogation room. "After what happened with us and that. . . thing. I don't think this is a good idea."

Ryan pulled back her freshly washed hair and tied it into a ponytail. The quivering in her chest hadn't stopped since she came out of that spirit walk where she'd dragged Holbrook from the clutches of the elemental. But she'd saved Matt—she could save Chad.

The man who sat tethered to the interrogation table was lost, too. That thing had taken him, like it had Holbrook and so many others over the years. Lost in a mansion to what they called the Beast. What do you call a creature that eats souls and manipulates people like Chad?

She had to do something to help him, or he could be lost forever.

"I can't leave him like this," Ryan murmured.

Holbrook's voice softened. "I owe you my life. It's just that I'm scared for you. I know what happened in there. What you saw. With whom you came in contact. I don't want that for you again." He placed a hand on her arm. "We don't want to lose you."

Ryan straightened her back. She pressed her hand to his chest, then handed him her watch—her lifeline to Lazarus. "Hold onto this for me. But I want it back when I'm done."

He nodded, but his face was pale. No one else could understand what they had experienced in Purgatory. Except Chad.

She turned and paced toward the interrogation room where Dave waited for her. Coti had already set up Lazarus, and he was there to get the device started. They exchanged a quiet nod and then entered the room.

Inside, Chad Harrison sat slumped over the table, wrists cuffed, eyes dead and distant. But she knew better now: *It* was watching her through him, as it had through Holbrook. The thing had used this young man to destroy everything the boy had, everything he was. Now, she was in this room again, facing the conduit for this evil.

By the time she had sat across from the boy, the temperature had become so cold that frost spidered across the edges of the two-way mirror. Chad's head lifted. His eyes—flat, inhuman— tracked her every breath. It remembered her.

She felt the familiar tug and suddenly understood. This was the same creature, infinite and everywhere. Like pieces of a whole broken into different bodies. One in Chad. One in Doc, when it had him. But all part of the hive mind.

"You know why I'm here," she said evenly.

Chad tilted his head to the right, studying her, dark pupils growing wide even in the harsh fluorescent lights.

She leaned closer, voice low. "You *will* give me Chad, or I'll rip him from you."

The thing laughed—a gurgle, thick and guttural, like

sewage bubbling up through a drain. Its breath was as foul and black as its form. Then it did something unexpected. It spoke. "Is that a threat?"

Her fist tightened, and she fought to keep her voice even. "A promise."

It laughed again, a sound that crawled over her body. "We are awaiting your return, then. I welcome it."

Her fingernails burrowed into the flesh of her palms. *Enough!* She should never have spoken to this thing.

"Dave. Now."

The keyboard clicked, and the blue grid flickered to life. Just before she shut her eyes, Chad's eyes filled with a sea of black.

The familiar thick fog of Purgatory clung to her skin, wrapping around her ribs and feet like claws. But this time, she didn't flinch. The black door waited in front of her, the silver knob pulsing like a heartbeat, making her skin crawl. It was too easy. A trap, and she knew it—but she had no choice.

Purgatory appeared empty as Ryan stood alone in this gray, swirling mass. But beyond the door, she knew *something* waited.

She grasped the handle and turned. The door creaked open, revealing a room different than the one where she'd found Doc. No bright blue ceramic tiles. A black box with floor-to-ceiling red claw marks gouged into the walls.

Chad sat huddled in the far corner, arms wrapped around his knees, eyes wide and terrified. The black entity filled the room, squirming like black vines from the corner, seeping into his skin, and infecting everything it touched. It tore through the walls, ripping at the paint.

Of course, it knew she was coming. It had dared her to come. But she knew its secret now and how to free its hostage.

Ryan crossed the floor in three strides and thrust her hand toward him. "Chad. I'm getting you out of here."

He staggered to stand, but the tendrils lashed out and slammed him into the wall. One coiled for her ankle. She dodged its grasp and stomped hard on the next that tried to wrap around her leg. The entity screeched and recoiled. She could injure it, and that's all that she needed Chad to see. She moved beyond the reach of another tendril and snapped a branch that pulled at her waist. Chad broke out of its hold and ran toward her. She grabbed his hand and they raced toward the door as the elemental roared.

But another figure filled the doorway, with a shape she hated more than death itself. Sam. Smiling. Whole. Alive in the dark that shouldn't exist. She wasn't going to let him get into her head this time.

Ryan stopped short, pulling Chad close to her. "Close your eyes, Chad, and hold onto me," she whispered, wrapping him in a tight embrace. She held his head to her shoulder, and his strong arms clung around her waist. "No matter what—don't let go."

"Okay." Chad whimpered, his arms trembling.

"Not this time," Sam hissed. Fingers like iron closed around her arm, yanking her back against his body. His breath raked against her neck, and she smelled the grave in it.

Sam wrapped a forearm around her throat. Her eyes flew open.

In that instant, Chad fell away from her so fast that she lost her grip.

Nooooo!

Then everything fell into darkness . . .

A flash of harsh light burst into her sight . . . then she fell back in her chair. The bright fluorescent lights of the interrogation room burned into her eyes as the headache from the electromagnetic pulse slammed into the base of her skull. She'd been pulled out of Lazarus too soon, and the disorientation left her vision swimming.

Too many voices. Not just Coti and Dave. Something was wrong.

She hit the floor as her chair was pulled aside by someone in a dark suit. From the cold linoleum, she could only watch as someone wheeled Dave out, powerless to stop it. More dark-clad men entered, walked past her, and unshackled Chad from the table.

The sounds around her were muffled and warped. Dave hadn't shut Lazarus down; she was *pulled* out prematurely. She could hear him yelling her name from the hallway. Ryan tried to clear her head by shaking it, but that only exacerbated the problem. When she managed to get to her feet, the men brushed her aside as they strode past, and in the middle of their tight formation shuffled Chad Harrison, wrists cuffed and a white cloth covering his head.

"Stop—" she shouted, her voice roaring in her head. "What are you doing? I'm not finished interrogating him yet. I'm not—."

They didn't care, but continued to push past her and into the hallway with Chad in the center of a six-man group. She stumbled after them, but a wall of muscle blocked her, hand firm on her shoulder. He wore the standard military-esque buzz cut and expressionless sunglasses—government, but not her department.

These weren't police, and they certainly weren't Finn's agents.

"Special Agent Mills," he said calmly. "We'll take the prisoner from here."

She pushed against his arm. "I'm not finished with him. You don't know what you're doing—he needs me." Her words stuck in her throat. Chad was still trapped inside—lost and alone. Without her help, he could be lost forever.

The man's mouth barely curved. He stared at her for several moments and then turned to follow the group down the hall.

"Excuse me! Who the hell are you?" she shouted, fumbling for the badge around her neck and flashing it at his retreating back. "I'm Special Agent Ryan Mills, SPECTER Division, and I have jurisdiction here!"

He stopped and turned slightly to deliver his final words. "Not anymore." Then he was gone.

"Under whose authority are you confiscating him?" Ryan lunged after them. More agents and uniforms poured into the hallway, staring. She shoved through the station doors and out into the parking lot in time to see a black armored van swallow the team and Chad. The doors slammed shut, the engine roared, and the van sped off into the dawn.

Ryan sank to her knees on the cold asphalt. The cool breeze whipped strands of hair that stuck to the tears on her cheeks. She'd failed him. Chad was lost forever to the elemental, all because some government agency wanted to protect its jurisdiction.

Coti, Agent Finn, and Colter stepped beside her, following her gaze as the taillights faded.

"Who were those guys?" she asked Finn.

He shook his head, jaw tight. "No idea. I was hoping you would know."

The van turned a corner and vanished—and with it, Chad Harrison, still shackled to a monster only she knew how to fight.

And she would.

CHAPTER 30

"I'm sorry I didn't brief you on that, Agent Mills." Director Price's monotone voice streamed through the speakerphone at the center of the table. "Some matters must stay classified."

Ryan gritted her teeth, glaring at the black phone as if it could feel her rage.

"With all due respect, *sir*, I was in the middle of an active interrogation. It is imperative I see Harrison again."

"I'm afraid that's not possible."

She shot a sharp glance toward Holbrook, who stood across from her with his arms folded. He nodded—steadying her, or agreeing, she wasn't sure.

"Why not, sir?" she pressed, folding her arms over her chest.

Price cleared his throat, something he always did when buying time to spin a better deception. Ryan knew every note of his annoying habit.

"It's simply not possible, Mills. Now, I've sent a new case file to your inbox. There will be a debrief tomorrow at the usual time. You and your team are dismissed."

The line clicked dead.

Ryan's fist hit the table, sharp and loud. "Unbelievable! He's keeping us in the dark."

Around her, the orange glow of the Lazarus machine washed over her. At least they were back home, together, her team intact with no casualties. It could have ended so much worse.

Coti leaned against the glass panel. "Do you think he sent us there to confirm the possession? And then to swoop in and bag Harrison once he knew for sure?"

Ryan shrugged. "Maybe."

"Damn," Coti muttered. "Real *Men in Black* crap."

"So . . . does that make *us* part of the conspiracy?" Dave asked. "I mean, we work for *him*."

Holbrook took in a deep breath. "Excuse me, but what do you mean by the *Men in Black*?"

Coti raised her eyebrows. "Oh, come on, Doc. You're kidding, right? Aliens, secret government coverups, black suits?"

Holbrook blinked, then it clicked. "Ah. Yes, the movies."

Ryan released a rough laugh—more breath than humor—and slid down the wall until she sat on the floor, arms draped over her knees. The adrenaline hadn't left her veins. Somewhere out there, Price held a secret. Worse, there were people with enough clearance to rip her cases out from under her before she could save anyone.

There was something that she had known deep in her soul—an old truth that resided in her blood and bones. A dark spirit followed her. As if she'd been chosen. Not since she'd killed Sam, but much longer. Whether it was actually Sam or not, she wasn't sure. But the Beast knew about him and used it against her. Every day, she sensed it growing stronger, feeding on her hidden memories and fears.

She inhaled slowly, leaning her head back. One day, she'd drag it into the light—and end it for good.

Oh, how I wish he'd go away.

ABOUT THE AUTHOR

When she isn't delivering babies, Carrie Merrill is a prolific writer who has put pen to paper since the age of eight, when she wrote her first story about a dragon that lived in a cave across the river from her house in Idaho. A day has not gone by since that time when she didn't have a story floating around in her head.

The Devil's Playground is her eighth novel and the second book in the new and exciting **S.P. E.C.T.E.R. series**.

Her other works include her highly-praised **Angel Blade series**, *The Key, The Outlaw and The Treasure*, an exciting YA novel, that takes place in the old West and is filled with adventure, and the "...Vivid, creepy and intense!" paranormal thriller, *Time of Death: Not All Secrets Stay Buried.*

Merrill is currently a full-time OB/GYN in Wyoming with her six rescue cats when she isn't writing about the things that lurk in the dark.

Follow Carrie Merrill at **CarrieMerrill.com**

TIME of DEATH
Not all Secrets Stay Buried

Dr. Evan Jensen, a surgical resident at St. John's Hospital, is left comatose after a horrific car crash. Trapped between life and death, she senses a sinister presence with her. Awakening with devastating injuries, Evan's recovery is plagued by whispers, shadows, and waking nightmares. Are they from her damaged brain—or tied to the hospital's forbidden north wing, where a dark tragedy still lingers?

The Lazarus Project:
Someday, I Will Collect You Too

When gifted homicide detective Ryan Mills joins the FBI's secret SPECTER division, she's introduced to LAZARUS—a device that replays crimes from fragments of evidence. But a new case links to her sister's disappearance eighteen years ago, marked by a chilling message:

"Yesterday, upon the stair, I met a man who wasn't there."

Available everywhere books are sold